I0690984

# TWISTED TALES & MORE....

### HIRA MEHTA

VISHWAKARMA PUBLICATIONS VP

# TWISTED TALES & MORE...

First Edition - January, 2017

© Hira Mehta
hiramehta13@gmail.com

ISBN - 978-93-85665-58-5

All rights reserved
No part of this publications may be reproduced, transmitted, or stored in a retrieval system, in any form or by any means, electronic, mechanical photocopying, recording or otherwise, without the prior permission of the publisher.

Disclaimer
This is a work of fiction, Names, characters, places and incidents are either the product of the author's imagination or are used fictitiously and any resemblance to any actual person, living or dead, events or locales in entirely coincidental.

Published by:
**Vishwakarma Publications**
283, Budhwar Peth, Near City Post, Pune- 411 002.
Phone No: (020) 20261157 / 24448989
Email: info@vpindia.co.in
Website: www.vpindia.co.in

Cover
**Dhun Cordo**

Typeset and Layout
**Chaitali Nachnekar - Vishwakarma Publications**

This book is sold subjects to the condition that it shall not, by way of trade or otherwise, be lent, resold, hired out, or otherwise circulated, without the publisher's prior consent, in any form of binding or cover other than that in which it is published.

# Contents

Foreword | v

1. A true story of an unsung princess | 1

2. Wrong about love!!! | 5

3. Walk to freedom | 10

4. Cold truth | 15

5. Cheated | 20

6. Out in the cold | 23

7. Is silence really golden? | 27

8. Hatred is such a simple word | 31

9. The village pond | 36

10. The forgotten night | 40

11. From beyond the grave.. | 44

12. Frozen darkness | 51

13. Mixed-up death | 55

14. The folly of loving | 59

15. The whispering night | 64

16. Help us please | 70

17. Terror unleashed | 74

18. The ghostly manor | 78

19. It had to be, for better or worse | 82

20. Edge of insanity | 86

21. Tired of hurting | 91

22. Flames of shame | 96

23. The crushed rose | 99

24. A prank too far | 103

25. Twins in the ashes | 106

26. No remorse | 109

27. There is a ghost in the house | 112

28. She knew but.... | 116

29. Broken wings | 119

30. Kite in the sky | 122

31. A nonsensical story | 125

32. Kitchen circus | 128

33. Women driver? | 132

# Foreword

It all began with some out of the blue random thoughts, that began to flow in the middle of the night. From that day onwards, a pen and pad always lay open on my bedside. It's been a long journey of four years to get to this day. The stories are a snapshot collection of all the flashes I've seen on celluloid. Would the characters, the story lines, the sounds sound familiar? They would, as they are from somewhere deep inside and. from the crevices of my subconscious mind that has absorbed so many moments of film magic to flow onto paper as stories. Most of these stories are for my inspiration, my dear daughter, Jharna or "Jeenu" as I fondly call her, and her love for the unknown and blood soaked macabre films and television shows. This is also my way to say thank you to the film fraternity for the stories of friendship, laughter, love and death that made me laugh and cry, think and sometimes worry too.

Surprisingly, today I don't fear death. I have seen it standing on the steps to my house, next to my mom waving me goodbye on that fateful day. There she was standing in her favourite powder blue dress. Today she is nothing but a sigh. When a tragic accident took my Mom away from me, I was traumatized, but I still feel her warmth when I close my eyes, like a hug, enveloping my body. I realise that she is not gone, but she is my angel on my shoulder helping me to face each new day and inspiring me to live life more.

When I was born my grandmother was disappointed that I was not a boy and said "a patthar (stone) is born", to which my dad said "No, it's a diamond. She will be a diamond and shine all her life." Thus I was named Hira. This has remained at the back of my mind always and I wonder if I have lived up to it. I firmly believe in the saying that only a woman who is happy with herself, can make others happy and therefore I choose to keep motivating myself and my friends to explore new roads.

Thank you all, especially my kids, my awesomely creative sis Dinku (Dhun), my baby sis Ruby, my soul sister Damini and soul mate, Chintan for letting me be "just me' and not to forget my dear friends whose continuous belief in me makes me strive for more.

An incomplete bucket list of dreams and the many hands I want to shake of those who inspired me along the way. A die-hard Hindi film buff who wants to acknowledge Mr. Amitabh Bachchan, whose 'never say die attitude' has inspired me to continue to explore new avenues and live by the saying:

"Age is an issue of mind over matter and if you don't mind, it doesn't matter" ~ Mark Twain

A big salute to the film fraternity for celluloid stories of friendship, laughter, love and death that inspired this poem:

# Lights, camera, action

Lights, camera, action, planning for each shot
Snow under the feet, green fields, its cold- it's hot!
Rehearsals, retakes, hard work, over and over again
There goes the light, here comes the rain

Swing the hip, slap that face, forget the pain
Spray your face, dab war paint, start again
Dangling from a wire, jumping over fire
Falling from a tree top and crying over a pyre.

Tears flowing- stop!  Now laugh a little more
Much more punch needed here for sure
Change the angle, pan to the side, and cut the light,
Slightly wide, to the left now little to the right,

Hello, you out there, just get out of the frame
Hang on the cliff, now on the roof of the train
Make-up, costumes, fittings and props
Make believe villages, houses and shops

Editing, post-production, final cut, edit done

Now's the time to find a place under the sun

Friday release, will it be a hit or flop

Bated breaths till the curtain drops

Back to the storyboard - once again!

Another film to plan. For the glory and the fame


I just pray that I can say with pride:

"When I stand before God at the end of my life, I would hope that I would not have a single bit of talent left, and could say, 'I used everything you gave me'." ~ Erma Bombeck

# 1

# A true story of an unsung princess

They had shifted in the two flats opposite mine, not that I cared. I was too busy with my life, to bother. Sometimes they smiled and I smiled back as I got in or out of the lift. That's all. Many a time fighting noises reached our ears and often I would just look through the peep hole to see the two women of the house fighting with the door open. One might think that being named a princess, Rajkumari would be treated like one by the family. The unmarried and uneducated Rajkumari was a sore point in the house, often ill-treated as she fought for money from her brother who denied her the simple things, she demanded. One day the money stopped for Rajkumari and the two flats that were one became two again. A small portion became Rajkumari's home while the rest of the flat area was engulfed by the sister-in-law, who closed the door on her. Rajkumari, deprived of money, soon took to walking the streets. She never used the lift and each day she walked down the seven stories of the building her perfume lingering on the staircase. Perhaps that's why, the fights were happening in the first place, I guess. Everyone turned against her as she dressed up each night to walk the streets only to return early morning. One fine day the family moved.

The story should have ended there but it did not. When her brother left the country, and the little or no money that came from him stopped, Rajkumari, troubled with her life, turned crazy by the day. Past midnight we would hear shouting and banging noises. We opened our door to find Rajkumari pounding crazily on the closed door of the other flat, screaming obscenities. She claimed that they were troubling her, and were hiding inside. I gently pointed to the big lock on the door telling her that the flat was locked and no one was inside, but to no avail. Days turned into months and the night disturbances continued as she pounded the door each night, shouting to them to come out and face her. The wooden door was scratched and destroyed each night and soon all kinds of presumably black magic items were found hanging on the door knob. She never troubled me but often caught me in the hallway to complain, as I tried to explain that no one was behind those closed doors. She refused to believe that, even though a big lock hung there ominously. The lock, she said, was just a ruse to get her to believe they were not inside. They were pounding on her walls from inside their flat she said. Things in her house were falling by themselves and she heard noises forcing her to come out. Things turned worse as time passed, and soon, to save the wooden door from getting wrecked completely, a big iron door was fitted, but did that stop her? No way! It made matters worse for us with louder noises of pounding on an iron door now.

One afternoon, I found her sitting on the jamb of the door peeling vegetables. "Didi didi," she said, "see they have cut the electricity now". I was appalled at her state. No electricity in the house, she was forced to sit with the door open of her flat to get the light from the passage to prepare her evening meals. Her flat door began to remain open for most part of the day with her sitting there. For me, she soon became my loving watchdog. Each day she would brief me on the ongoings of my flat. She would tell me when my kids came home, who else knocked, and so on. I warmed up to her slowly as I realized that she had never in the past so many years ever troubled us or my growing kids. In fact she became their caretaker who fussed over them each time they opened the door. I came home many an evening to be told by my daughter that she had given Rajkumari cold water to drink during the hot summer days. I never had the courage to do much and I wonder why. Maybe I was just too busy in my own life. A cheerful, "How are you today didi?" became my daily evening greeting, and I responded to her warmth too. Days turned to months. Soon, I began to miss her, coming home to a closed door and often wondered why. Maybe, I thought, my timing was just not right. But then I was shocked to know that she had been thrown out of the flat on the streets. "We have growing children," they said "and she was the 'bad influence'". Maybe they were right in their own way. When I enquired where she had gone, they seemed most unconcerned and uncaring. I could not sleep for days wondering where Rajkumari must have gone. Uneducated, not able to write a word in any language and penniless, she was out there alone in the world.

Life went on as usual and each day I got out of the lift, I would stare at the closed door and wonder how or where she could be. I remembered the day she had rung the doorbell and asked me to keep her jewellery safe for her. I had refused suggesting that she better put it in a bank or with someone in the family. I remember much later, she had told me, that she had been duped of that too. Then one day I knew. My heart stopped as I could not believe what I was hearing. Rajkumari was dead. She was dead? When, how? She was found dead on the footpath one night unattended and alone, and as I write this I can see her gentle face smiling at me. The house has changed hands since then many a times, but till date no one who has bought it has ever come to stay. I curse myself often for not being there to help her or even trying. But then, how could I have known? I knew she was not stable mentally. I curse her family who had abandoned her and believe me, I was not a bit unhappy to hear that her sister in law passed away just a month after Rajkumari, of a heart attack. They say our sins do not leave us and the Gods must have truly loved the gentle Rajkumari to bring her sister in law to stand before her, up there in the clouds.

2

# Wrong about love!!!

The words began to blur on the newspaper she held, as Julie's eyes glistened with tears. She sat up painfully in the bed, reminded once again, of the old injuries that never seemed to heal. Her thoughts flew back to the day she had stepped out onto the dance floor for the first time. That day, she knew she was born to dance. Her mother, Melody, a street dancer, could not afford to send her to dance school so she would play the gramophone at home, and they both would dance together. Soon, times changed and Melody became famous and the stage became her home. Coiled like a snake waiting to spring, she waited for school to end and then shot out like an arrow to the dance class with Zeena. Dancing was their only passion. Zeena, her dearest friend with light brown eyes was lively, outspoken, but totally scared of spiders while Julie on the other hand was dependable, moody and always scared of being let down. Totally different in many ways, they were always partners in crime and they had a secret dream, a dance school of their own.

She paused to hold her fluttering heart as she spotted him. He sat there in the second row, his dark brown eyes on her, following her every move. Arjun, tall, dark and handsome was the man she dreamt of. He was much more and had walked straight into Julie's heart. "She is going to kill me, but whether she likes it or not Arjun will be mine soon," thought Zeena, her eyes narrowing with hatred, as she watched them walking hand in hand along the sea shore. The three friends often huddled around the table over steaming coffee, drawing up plans of their dream dancing school. They were not going to dance behind the lead dancer anymore. Zeena wanted to call it 'Julzee', a combination of both their names, and Arjun wanted to call it Swirls & Twirls. Julie, bemused, had watched them argue over the name. She knew who she was going to name after. It had to be Melody, her mother's name. A perfect name and what better tribute to remember her mother, who left her the cute little studio with its high ceilings. After all, it was she who had put up with all her tantrums, the late coming, and it was she, who had gotten father to agree to let her dance.

The studio was at last ready and painted. The walls were covered with mirrors, and the floors were shinning new. Julie watched the carpenters tap the last few nails into the wooden floor. The studio soon became one of the most sought after dance schools and then came that one chance that they had been waiting for. A chance to perform for the biggest show of their lives and Julie was enthralled! But then it happened. It just was not to be. A man on a motorcycle went onto the wrong side of the road, hit the curb, flew in the air and came back down hard on the bonnet, sending her spinning onto the curb. Nursing broken bones and feeling sorry for herself, she watched Arjun and Zeena, as they regaled her with stories of the preparations for the show. This was just what she had been waiting for. Zeena knew now that the time was just right for her to worm her way into Arjun's heart. She sat closer to Arjun caressing him gently with her fingers and smiling seductively and hanging on to his every word. Arjun seemed to enjoy the attention and Julie's weary eyes did not miss the gentle touches, loving looks exchanged so often between the two. As they left the hospital room, she struggled to the window and hid in its shadows. There they were standing entwined in the dark shadow of the tree. She watched Zeena melt into his arms as Arjun kissed her gently. Arjun would not do this to her after all he loved her, but she could not ignore what she was seeing. She lay back in her bed too drugged to protest. Her broken body would not let her move and slowly the smile on her face disappeared. She was not going to grovel before her best friend, or, was she really her best friend? Maybe Zeena would get over him, let him go or maybe he will realise, but she knew it could never be the same again.

Her mind began to play games with her as she lay there staring at the white ceiling. She had lost everything in the accident and she cursed the man who crashed into her. The anger inside her, buried deep, was coming alive and kicking up a storm. Arjun belonged to her and if she could not have him, neither could Zeena. She knew now that she had lost him forever. As they say revenge is a dish best served cold. It had to be done and Julie wondered whether her conscience would allow her to do whatever was needed to stop them. Zeena's moves became bolder by the day as if she dared Julie to get out of bed and stop her. She watched them silently as she lay there broken on the bed. Arjun, had begun to avoid her gaze. Zeena, her childhood companion and partner in crime! "How could she?", she thought. She lay there and bid her time. Back on her feet, consumed with anger and jealousy, she ran her plan a hundred times over in her mind. Anyway, an accident during the grand celebration of the successful show on the high seas would not require too much of careful planning. After all, she knew that Zeena did not know how to swim. It was not going to be an ordinary evening of fun for sure, thought Julie.

7

Everyone was having fun but her, as she sat there twirling the crutch in her hand. She sat there watching them dancing on the open deck as the sun slowly sank its rays shining its goodbyes to the tiny waves lashing gently against the swaying ship. The voices grew louder and the party noisier as the laughter filled the air. Julie nursed her drink twirling the glass in her hand watching them. Her eyes turned cold as she watched Zeena sit down on the high stool leaning against the railings, smiling invitingly at Arjun. "The moment is right", thought Julie. Slowly she got up and closed in on Zeena before Arjun could reach her. Accidentally brushing against the frenzied students and pretending to lose control of her crutch was all she had to do. She watched a few youngsters topple over like skittles against Zeena's high stool throwing her over into the water. She screamed for help, as she hurtled into the dark night sea. No one seemed to know what had hit her. Loud screams rended the air, as everyone ran towards the railings, peering into the water searching the dark waters for her. Arjun froze, turned to stone as he turned to look at Julie, not willing to believe what he thought he saw. An evil smile curled as Julie lifted her glass in a mock salute and hobbled over to the railings to peer into the dark sea. All hell had broken loose. The boatman dived into the dark water swimming furiously towards her. They all watched with bated breath peering into the dark waters as the boatman battled the choppy sea swimming towards her. She thrashed her arms in the water, trying to keep herself afloat. The dark grey waves seemed to carry her further away each time as the boatman struggled in the darkness trying to reach her. They watched and egged on the boatman pointing towards her and begging him to reach her. The screams became lounder as Zeena's clothes turned into heavy weights dragging her to the depths of the endless sea. The darkness of the night seemed to have taken a fancy to their victim, Zeena, and the grey waves splashed higher pulling her deeper and deeper into its depths.

Exhausted from fighting the waves, Zeena began to slowly give up and sank into the dark waters, the current too strong for her. Soon the bobbing head of Zeena disappeared into the dark sea, as the boatman took deeper breaths diving down lower and lower searching for her. Then all was silent.

Days melted away into months, and into years, and soon, the accidental death of Zeena was a thing of the past. Julie had continued to run the studio, while Arjun blaming her for Zeena's death , had stormed out of her life. In the end, it didn't matter to her anymore. She had taken her revenge and no one had realised the truth. Her frozen heart did not care anymore, as she turned cold with hatred. Arjun had married and his rich wife's mad schemes of making more money had hit rock bottom. Serves him right, she thought as she listened to stories of his failed marriage and business. She had thought, Arjun was a strong man, who, no woman could bring on his knees; but he had proved her wrong. This wasn't where he wanted to be, she thought. Long dried up tears welled up and as the paper dropped to the floor, her tearful eyes read, "Bankrupt entrepreneur kills wife and commits suicide leaving behind large debts".

●●●

3

# Walk to freedom

Shanta smiled at the rapt faces in her classroom as they leaned forward, their little hands under their chin, listening to her soft voice reading aloud. She smiled indulgently at her daughter, huddled over her books with the rest of her class, her soft brown curls blowing against her forehead. As Shanta gathered her books to leave the classroom, her thoughts flitted back to the day she had walked home from school, straight into the arms of Amma waiting impatiently at the doorway. As Amma dragged her into the courtyard, Shanta caught a fleeting glimpse of a tall dark heavily mustached gentleman puffing away at the hookah sitting on the green charpoy next to Appa; "and who was that fat ugly woman?" she wondered, as she pulled back to get a better glimpse. Dragging her in furiously, Amma muttered to herself as she quickly pulled out a green and red sari and matching the jewelry with it. Muttering furiously, Amma stripped Shanta of her uniform and packed her off to bathe. Shanta sat down palms folded looking down at her feet stifling her giggles and stealing glances at the two most humongous human beings she had ever seen in her life. "God help," she thought, "Amma can't be seriously thinking of sending me to their home". Shanta lowered her eyes as Amma cocked her head with pride, and enveloped her daughter in a bear hug.

That night, Shanta put her head in Amma's lap and cried. She did not want to get married, she was only sixteen. Not to this man anyway. He was much older than her and she hated him. She wanted to become a teacher and besides what if she did not give that family a son? "Look at what happened to my friend Vanshika", she begged Amma. How could she forget her running out of the house on fire, as the crowd at the chowraah of the village stood watching? Vanshika's screams still rang in her ears, as she remembered running out with a blanket trying to save her dearest friend, gasping in her arms, her eyes imploring Shanta for help. Everyone said the stove turned over, but she never believed it for a minute, as it she was who had heard Vanshika's moan, "they burnt me!", and close her eyes forever. She could still feel the pressure of her hand holding on tightly, as Vanshika gasped in pain. She did not want to end up like her. Amma stroked her head and wailed along with her, but Appa would not budge. Soon everything was silent, as Shanta stood on the terrace staring at the million stars above, praying for a miracle.

The smell of sandalwood filled the air, as pattering feet ran wildly across the courtyard. The sound of the flute hurt her nerves, and so did the fragrance from the thalis filled with jasmines, roses and mogras.. Lush green banana leaves flanking the pandal corners, waving in the soft breeze, as the pot-bellied pundit tied them tight to the posts. Teary-eyed, Shanta sat looking out of her window as her friends sat around her fussing. 'Ready for the kill', thought Shanta, as hot tears fell on her outstretched hands amidst chiding from Velluriba working furiously at the mehendi. The wafts of sweets melting in the earthen pots mingled with the aromas that could appease the Gods, but not Shanta, as she stared tear-eyed at the pundit stoking the fire. Loud burst of crackers announced the arrival of the groom and soon it was all over.

As Vishnu Prasad reached for his bride, she recoiled in horror. Every night when all were asleep, she ran up to the terrace and looked up to the stars to implore Vanshika to help her and then she started to cry. She did not have the strength to run away. Then came that day, when Shanta's heart filled with fear and an unexplained anticipation. She was worried and happy, as she placed her hand on her stomach, feeling the heart beat of her little one. Somehow she knew it was going to be a girl and as she looked across at Vishnu Prasad working at his desk, she promised herself no matter what, she was not going to end up burnt on the chowraah. "It could not be happening again", he thought, as he stared at the reports. First Vanshika and now Shanta, both had failed him. Vishnu Prasad was furious, but he knew they could not make it look like an accident anymore.

Vishnu Prasad was a loving husband and a much respected man, so the villagers refused to believe that he tortured Shanta in the confines of the bedroom,

How could they suspect? Soon stories about her clandestine outings in the night horrified the village. She had a lover and was bearing his child. He called the panchayat, while his parents so magnanimously agreed to forgive her. She tried telling her mother, it was a son they wanted, but the stony eyes of a woman trapped in rituals stared back at her. The whispers grew, that she was ashamed of her deeds and had tried to end her life many a times. Shanta knew she was trapped, as she watched him laugh lying in the confines of the dark basement of the house. They starved her for days and she knew it would not be long before something happened to her unborn.

12

The villagers watched and waved as the cart jumped over the muddy track towards the hills to the temple steps. They were taking her there to atone for her sins before the lord. Shanta caressed the little one in her womb, her eyes following the clouds running alongside, as if trying to say something to her. Soon they started the climb to the temple, higher and higher, each step under her foot scorching her soles and the stones pricking her feet as if urging her to stop. The sun was setting slowly and the skies turning dark. The steps were getting emptier and emptier, as the devotees walked past them climbing down towards the village chanting loudly. Gasping for breath, her mother-in-law stopped and sat down on the ledge beckoning Shanta to sit next to her. Shanta stood, turned to stone, as a chill ran down her spine. Something was not right, she thought as she stared at the flight of empty steps of the temple. The dark skies, the mossy gloomy steps to the temple dome loomed way ahead. She knew she had to run, but they were watching her closely and there was nowhere to run anyway. Why were they standing so close to the edge of the cliff, she thought trying to pull away from her mother-in-law's tight clasp? The breeze caressed her hot cheeks, as she stood there wondering what to do. She looked up at the looming temple in the far distance, praying for help and saw someone standing there. It could not be, she thought, as she peered into the dark shadows at the familiar figure standing on the steps there beckoning her. "I must be tired, it must be just my imagination', she thought standing there feeling giddy. She gulped at the warm breeze, her heart beats quickening, as she tried to unclasp the hand that held on tight. Her eyes rolled in horror, as her husband suddenly reached out to push her over the edge. It could be happening she thought, as she felt her body float like a feather in the soft breeze and fall to the side as if someone had pushed her gently out of the way. Her eyes clouded, as she heard her in-laws scream, as they watched their son's body hit the trees

13

below. An unexplainable warmth engulfed her. Vanshika stood there holding out her hand to Shanta, slowly pulling her up, gently touching her cheek to fade away, waving goodbye, as tears rolled down Shanta's cheeks.

That night the police came and took them away. In the still of the night, she stood on the terrace for the last time looking up to the stars. "Vanshika, my dear friend, thank you", said Shanta, as she walked away forever.

●●●

4

# Cold truth

Ansi gasped in pain, as it shot through her stomach. "Oh no", she thought "my baby!". Her mother was right, she shouldn't have insisted on coming for the wedding. Where were they going to find a doctor in this god-forsaken hometown of her mother-in-law? As the old rattling taxi droned into the highway of the hospital, Mansi felt a chill run down her spine. This dark black monstrous building, surrounded by dark pathways, cannot be a hospital. It looked like a house on horror street. Maybe they were at the wrong place, and what were those stone steps with ancient statues doing in a hospital?. This did not seem the place, her mother-in-law suggested they take her to. "Not a soul in sight, they don't even have a watchman at the iron gate,", she thought, as they just turned into the pathway. The taxi driver too seemed nervous and scared as he kept looking over his shoulder at Mansi. Dark green curtains fluttered in the breeze on the windows like hands outstretched as if beckoning them. "How silly am I, worrying for nothing", thought Mansi, as she clutched her husband's hand tight and walked into the hospital.

Empty beds lay marching in a row except for one in the far corner. She smiled at the sleeping woman on the bed. Mansi did not like the place at all, it was so dreary and dusty. As she lay down trying to sleep, the white curtains waved high above her head as if trying to tell her something. The dark shadows of the branches of the tree outside her window fell on her pillow, as if reaching out to grab her while the cold wind touched her face gently caressing her. She closed her eyes hoping that they would leave her alone.

Mansi groaned and turned over, trying to sleep on the lumpy mattress. A small smile flitted across her face, as the little one turned in her stomach. They had already decided his name, 'Akaash'. "Girls were cursed in their family", he had said. So deciding a name was out of the question. Besides daughters had never survived in this family, but then how could anyone be so sure? She wondered, what if it were a girl instead? Her eyes dropped and as she turned to look down the hallway at the large mahogany desk sitting there forlorn. "Where was the matron? And shouldn't someone be sitting on the desk watching over them?", she wondered, but then there were only two of them in the empty rows of beds. Maybe she was in some other ward, tending to others. The next morning she spent her time counting the empty iron beds around her, and talking to Raashi. Raashi, the beautiful young girl with a smile that lit up the room, who had asked to be moved to the bed next to her. Mansi tossed and turned trying to sleep waking up to Raashi's painful groans. Shantabai's eyes bore into her very being as she wheeled off Raashi, groaning in pain.

The shadows on her bed turned golden as the warm breeze caressed her awake. Raashi lay on the bed next to her, cuddling her baby boy. They spent the whole day talking and laughing each time the little boy punched his fisted hands about as if trying to touch the stars. Morning came and Mansi opened her eyes, heavy like lead, her head spinning and painful. The beds were empty and there was no one left but her in the maternity ward. Where was Raashi, after all, she had delivered her baby just yesterday? "Oh! Raashi?" The doctor said, "She has gone home. In the middle of the night. Shantabai saw that the baby had turned blue. We tried everything but he died". "No that cannot be", she argued, "that is not possible, everything was fine yesterday, and who sends a woman home next day after delivery? Something is not right, I know. How come I slept through all this? Take me home from here", she begged of her husband as she stared at her mother-in- law hiding in the shadows.

The pains came in stronger and stronger, and it was not long before Mansi lay in bed cuddling her newborn son. Tucking her in, Shantabai whispered slowly in her ear, 'This place is haunted, and neither you nor your son will survive. Leave before it is too late'. "Oh boy!" thought Mansi, "Is she actually talking to me?."

She stifled a pretended scared giggle, and called her closer, begging for more. "Tarita, was only twenty," said Shantabai, "born into a house where girl child is a curse on the society and where girls are told that they are inferior and a burden for the family. Tarita, saw her mother slave over the stove day in and day out. Her father was an educated man, but when it came to traditions, he could not see beyond the hair of his moustache. Then one day the television came into the house, and Tarita cuddled up with her mother each afternoon, as the moving pictures slowly unfurled the modern woman. She would revolt against her father in her mind and dream the impossible dream of freedom. Her heart revolted, her soul revolted, her mind too, and each night, Tarita lay on her bed, wishing she had the courage to speak her mind. But next morning, things were just the same. Then one day she was married off much against her wishes and soon, she was pregnant and her mother-in-law insisted she find out whether it was a girl or a boy. Better kill

17

a female fetus, she said, rather than give birth to an unwanted child. If a daughter is killed, the next child will be a son, she explained to the flabbergasted Tarita. A screaming Tarita was dragged here, to this very room. Her mother-in-law pressed a few hundred rupee notes in the hand of the doctor as they wheeled her into the room. She cried and begged them not to touch her little unborn girl, but they would not listen. I couldn't do anything but wipe the sweat from her brow. Tarita screamed that she would not let them get away, that she would take revenge on all those laughing at her as she slowly slipped into unconsciousness and a few days later heartbroken, into an unwanted death. I watched it all happen, but I could do nothing but watch them take her away covered in a blanket of white," continued Shantabai, "I could not sleep or rest for days after that incident and then one day I peeped into her home. They seemed to be happy she was gone. The neighbours told me they were looking for a new bride for their son."

"Soon, footsteps could be heard walking down the corridors of the hospital at night. Some say they saw the shadow of a young woman smiling, and sometimes she turned horrendously ugly. The birth of a boy meant sure death in the hospital. Many a times, I have seen Tarita walking the corridors," said Shantabai. "No one comes here anymore. Why did you come, didn't your mother-in-law warn you?" Mansi stifled a giggle, as she looked at Shantabai in surprise. "You know my mother-in-law? Rubbish, I don't believe this. There are no such things as ghosts." Her expression slowly turning into fear as the old woman's face suddenly seemed possessed by a demon, eyes glazed and unflinching. Shantabai stood there, clutching the corner of her sari twirling it nervously. Mansi panicked but no one was there and as she reached for the bell, Shantabai yanked it out of her hand and pushed her down hard onto the pillow raving and ranting, "I knew Tarita would return, she had promised revenge. She would come to avenge her girl's death,' she screamed, "She would avenge the death of my girls too". Mansi eyes rolled in horror as she cried out "Your girls?".

"Yes, yes" the old woman shouted "they killed them in my womb, even before they were born, two of them, one after the other, like I was just a child bearing machine. The third time, I ran away to my village. They could not kill her in my womb, so they came when she was born and in the darkness of the village night strangled her, beat me up, and threw me into the well to die. I died a thousand deaths, waiting for them to leave. I knew they would come back, but the well was not new to me and they did not know that. I had played hide and seek in that well as a kid. I dragged myself out, and I dug my daughter's grave with my own hands. Foolish me, returned home and begged for another chance but shocked to see me alive, they beat me over and over again and threw me out of the house. Do you know what they did after that? They brought him a new wife. I waited and watched praying hard for her to have the same fate, but she delivered a son. A son! Yes! A son! And did I try to get to him? Many a time, but he escaped me. They feared for him, so they sent him away far over the seven seas out of my reach. Do you know which woman took my place? Your mother-in-law. Yes, yes!! She saved your husband from me, but look! She sent you here to die instead, and so you will", she cried, "You will die, and so will your son, just as did Raashi's son and all the other boys born here". "No! No!" Mansi screamed, "Don't do this! Let me go!" Mansi's body thrashed about as Shantabai laughed, and soon the pillow muffled her screams forever.

●●●

5

# Cheated

Reema stared in disdain at the old woman in the pale grey sari, sitting at the window blissfully unaware, rubbing the peanuts in her palms. The skins flew back into the hall with a waft of breeze from the window. "Who said it's all about loving your elders?" she thought. "It's about living with them, especially her," she thought, picking up the mess she was making. She never left them alone, always hovering around them and never letting her be. "All mothers-in-law are the same," she thought. "They just love being the spoke in wheel of marriage."

Then one day, Radha aunty walked into the house, bags and all, as Reema stared, with her mouth open. That night, they fought after a long time. Reema accused her husband of not even informing her. "Why did Radha Aunty need to come? Could he have not have taken the old woman for the check-up?" she screamed into the night like a banshee. Outside in the hall, Radha Aunty stared at the cringed face of her sister sitting with folded hands, head downcast. Reema flounced around the bedroom, making up that extra bed, organizing the house to accommodate an additional person refusing to talk to anyone, and ignoring Radha Aunty. Days passed as the two women made visits to the doctor, but she did not care or bother to ask.

When Reema returned from work that evening, a shiver ran down her spine, at the deafening silence in the house. "This is unusual," she thought. "They wouldn't go anywhere, Where would they go so late?", she wondered. How inconsiderate of them to not inform her, but then she too was not going to call and ask where they were. They should have told her if they were going to be home late. She would wait for an hour or so and then call Sameer; she fumed, as she paced the floors wanting to scream blue murder. She sprang up like a coiled cobra ready to attack, as the latch turned, but she was not prepared for what she saw. An ashen faced Radha Aunty was holding onto the old woman's arm, and as she lay her sister down on the bed, she heard Radha Aunty mutter as tears rolled down her face "it's a deadly tumor, but there is hope". Reema reeled back in shock as a deep pain shot through her.

Reema had been just eighteen, and in love, and he too truly loved her. Long walks on the beach, those romantic nights together, and soon with a promise to return to marry her, he left her waving goodbye as she watched the train take him far away. At first he came over the weekends, then slowly the visits stopped, and then the calls stopped. She called him several times but he did not return her calls. She waited and waited in vain and could take it no more. One day she just landed at his doorstep. He stood before her, unashamed at cheating her and his wife. He had played with her feelings, cheated her for the two years while all the while she had built castles in the air. He had never told her the truth about the tumor, he knew he had. He just wanted to live out all his fantasies and she was the one affair that he had wanted. The thrill of having another woman in his life before he died. He was not scared of dying, and never intended to come back. He had just wanted to have fun, live life to its fullest and do all the things he wanted. He had so many more things on his list and did not care if he left behind hurt and pain, after all, he was the one dying. Her parents had pleaded with her to bury his memories under the carpet, but it had not been easy for her to forgive herself for being such a fool. Then Sameer had come into her life, but she hid the past from him.

She had felt cheated and used then and now, once again the deadly virus had reared its ugly head in her life. How could she explain to them the guilt that was surfacing to eat away her peace? They knew nothing about Raj. It was her darkest secret, buried deep in her heart.

Reema could take it no more. Her heart cramped and she burst into tears falling at her feet. The old woman stroked her head as she begged forgiveness, talked about Raj, her broken dreams, her despair. Slowly and steadily, the storm ebbed into a peaceful silence in both their hearts, their eyes washed by tears, clearly seeing a new beginning. Sameer and Radha Aunty watched over them wrapped up in each other and smiled.

●●●

**6**

# Out in the cold

Drinking was my passion and I knew it would kill, but do I care? Life has not been good to me, then why should I worry about life. It was death I was interested in knowing better.

I still remember the first few drops of brandy that dropped down my tiny mouth. "Just two drops and his fever will go," said mother. That was the beginning; the taste had lingered on my mouth forever. I grew up watching father sit down on the broken armchair sharing the glass of golden liquid with mother. Many times, they allowed me to lick their fingers dipped in their glasses as they promised me my first drink when I turned eighteen.

It was my twelfth birthday party. I watched my uncles gulp down glasses of wine and whiskey, reaching for more each time the waiter passed by. Uncle Sam saw me staring longingly and winked as he weaved his way around the guests. "Want to taste some son?" he asked me. Did I want some!! I wanted it all, but dare not show it on my face. Uncle Sam smiled and held out the glass as I tried to keep a very straight face. "You won't like this too much, it's not juice you know, son," he said as I took the glass in my hand. It was actually happening! I had a glass of whiskey in my hand until that horrified scream snatched the glass away. "You wicked boy!", screamed mother glaring at Uncle Sam. I stared in horror as I watched my prey being taken away. This could not be happening! I had come this close to my fantasy.

That night I could not sleep. It was useless. I had to get to that bottle. I was not waiting anymore. I flung off the covers and tip toed out of the room to my parent's bedroom. They were fast asleep, but this was going to be tricky. Could I reach it without making noise? I had to try. I was desperate, and desperate times need desperate measures, they say. I got down on fours and slowly crawled toward the cupboard. "Will it creak?" I wondered as I gritted my teeth and gently nudged the door. It had to creak, I knew it would!! I ducked under the bed. They did not stir. "So far so good," I thought, as I opened the door and pulled out the bottle, its warm golden liquid swirling in the bottle so invitingly. I pulled out a glass gently, slowly uncapped the bottle and poured out some whiskey, or was it brandy? I could not read the label, and I didn't care. This was just divine and now I knew why it was called 'the drink of the Gods'. Just one swifter gulp, then another, and then it struck me. The glass would need to be washed. Why had I not thought of this before? I gently grabbed the edge of mother's bedcover, taking care not to pull it too much and wiped the glass clean. Gently as I placed it on the shelf along with the bottle, all hell broke loose as the glass cracked against the door.

Punished and walloped for my sin, I sat watching my parents scream, blaming each other for the outcome of their folly. I knew I would need to cry, and so I did bawling loudly, saying 'sorry' and 'forgive me' over and over and then falling on the ground feigning dizziness, until the sounds of their screams dimmed.

As I lay in bed, I realized how stupid I had been. I should have just taken the bottle and left. I decided that they would never catch me again and they never did. I turned eighteen, and that night dad gave me the car keys for the first time. He was proud of me, after all, I had graduated with top honors. It was my birthday too after all. That night I partied away into the wee hours of the night with Rohit, Asmit, Sheena and Susie. It was dawn, and we were not yet tired of our revelry. Drunk and happy, we decided to make it to the hills for a long drive.

I was in no state to drive, that I knew, but I was not going to let my friends think I was a naïve young man. One hand driving was easy but then why was the road in front of me so crooked and hazy? And why was everything turning black? A loud thud! An upturned car and then it was all over. Rohit groaned holding his bleeding head, Sheena lay on the floor of the car, like a broken doll. Asmit and Susie were not moving. My head was swimming and eyes were blurred. Drunken driving! Jailed for years and then thrown out of the house with nothing to call my own. I walked around, begging friends to let me stay in their house, but no one wanted to have anything to do with someone just out of jail. I was a sinner, responsible for the death of two lives. I knew I had to leave town.

The jail had not dimmed my addiction; I had taken plenty of it with the jail staff I had befriended. I needed money to drink. Now out and with nothing left, I knew I could not go stealing for long and maybe it was time to settle down in one place. Washing cars was not the job for me, but what else could I do? At least it paid me enough to drink. I ate and slept in the backyard of the petrol pump of an old Parsi man, Rustomji, a benevolent soul who heard my story and yet gave me a roof over my head. Every night I would sit around with the other mechanics drinking away my money. Rustomji stood at the window staring at me, his eyes boring into my soul, but I had nothing to live for. I did not care anymore. This was my life.

Death always comes slowly for those who sin, and who knew better than me? The pains kept recurring, and I couldn't get up and work anymore. I lay in the corner of the garage begging death to come. Each night I saw the darkened shadows glint on the tin roof. The walls seemed to close in on me, my legs felt like lead, my hands shook, my lips dried, crushed like autumn leaves and my head, it just never stopped pounding. I begged Rustomji for a drink, but he would not budge, pushing doses of medicine down my parched throat. Why won't he just let me die? I thought. Then one day he pulled out my jail papers and called my parents. I did not want them to come. I knew they were not going to anyway, but they came and cried till tears ran dry. "Let's go home, son!" Mom said, as she pulled me up, covering my thin bony shoulders in a warm engulf. Rustomji smiled as he hugged me goodbye, "You will make it, son. Life is a struggle", he said "it's only when we are no longer afraid, do we begin to live".

I can see the white ceiling above my bed, calm and peaceful and silent as the walls watched over me indulgently. My hands and legs are mine again, my lips blooming like soft petals, and my head is as clear as the blue sky outside my hospital window. I have been forgiven. Sheena and Rohit are there for me. I have my friends back. The computer on my table is beckoning me to finish my thesis. Life is beckoning. It's true that nobody gets to live life backwards and there will always be something, or some obstacle, in your way. Maybe something to be gotten through first, a debt to be paid. At last it has dawned on me that I chose to let death find me. Thankfully it was not too late to realize that life is a companion that goes along with us on a journey. I just did not know.

●●●

7

# Is silence really golden?

Masterji raised his hands in horror as Kishen bowed in front of him. "How many times have I told you not to do this!" he growled, "why don't you understand, it is this action of yours that makes you feel inferior to me". Grasping the bony shoulders, he lifted the farmer off the floor and bade him to sit next to him on the charpoy. Kishen's eyes brimmed with tears as he placed the letter in Masterji's hands. "See what my son has done to me", his shaky voice hiding his fear, "is this why I sent him to town? He is in jail for murder." Masterji read the letter, frowning and shaking his head.

Masterji always knew that Ramu was brilliant, and he had promised to bring technology to his village. Masterji could not understand why suddenly the lure of the town had made Ramu a criminal. He knew he would have to go to town and see for himself. The tonga ride seemed to go on forever, bumping erratically, as the thoughts running through his mind. Over a cup of tea, Rupesh broke the news to Masterji as gently as he could," I had to send that letter. Ramu is in jail for murder of his roommate Akaash". Masterji's hand shook and the cup spilled over as Rupesh told the story.

Akaash loved his work as a writer with a small printing press, and soon Ramu and Akaash had became the best of friends spending many a day sitting together on the charpoy sharing their dreams. Sharan, their other roommate was a loner who never seemed to be around.

Then one day, three men rented the empty room next door. The thin walls could not keep the discussions out, as more and more animated arguments over politics, discontent on inter-community fights and disagreements, continued late into the night. Sharan seemed to hit off with them and soon he was a part of their late night discussions. Akaash's writings became more and more aggressive as each night's discussion revealed the darker side of the three visitors next door. The thin walls kept nothing a secret, as Akaash placed a glass against the wall listening and taking notes. Ramu cautioned Akaash to stay away from writing about it to fill his newspaper pages, but it fell on deaf ears.

Then one dark dismal day in the hot summers, a disheveled Sharan, covered with dust, stuffed his bag into the cupboard and proceeded to wash himself. Akaash had been waiting for this moment. He rummaged in Sharan's bag, pulling out one of the many small round grey objects and dropped it back, shocked. Quickly hanging the bag back on the rusty nail, he retreated to the end of the corridor, and waited till Sharan and the bag disappeared next door. Akaash put his ear to the thin wall and sat down looking out into the dark silent street waiting for words to put to paper, whilst Ramu's silent eyes implored him not to write. That fateful night Akaash wrote for hours piecing together the snatches of voices he heard through the thin walls as Sharan and the three men sat together in the room eating and drinking.

The flash of the camera broke up the party and Akaash sprinted down the corridor into the dark street. Ramu watched melting into the shadows of the corridor unable to do anything, as they dragged Aakash back to the room. As soon as the key turned in the lock and they left, he sprinted out of the shadows calling out to Akaash, but there was no reply. Ramu tried pushing the window open, but it just did not budge no matter how hard he tried. Suddenly a hand covered his mouth from behind and he felt a sharp blow on his head as he struggled to get free. Down he went onto the floor falling on something wet and sticky. Struggling awake, he raised his bloody hand to the light of the moon and turned sick as the slit throat of Akaash gaped at him. He screamed and screamed till a blood stained cloth muffled his voice and tied him down. That night the men disappeared into the night.

The sunlight broke into the window as Ramu raised his aching head unable to see straight. "What was this dull ache in his throat and why was his tongue feeling heavy? How long had he been lying there?" he wondered. Sharan's unflinching gaze never left Ramu, as he dragged him and tied him to the bedpost. The police came and found Ramu sitting next to Akaash with a blood-stained knife in his hand. Sharan sobbed telling the tale of how he had overpowered the terrorist who had slit the throat of the unwitting writer.

The cell's cold stone bed froze his body, as Ramu lay shivering violently. His glazed eyes staring at small dingy cell and the other men huddled together over cold rice. The iron door with the uncaring bars creaked open. He raised his head and recoiled in horror. "It's them, the men from next door. What were they doing here? he thought and why were they dressed in uniforms. Oh God! They are the law," thought Ramu, as they closed in on him laughing, beating him till all went black.

"I went to meet him but they never allowed me to meet him. I don't know how he is or what they have done to him, that's why I called for you, Masterji", said Rupesh. Masterji reached shakily for his stick, eyes blurred as he cried silent tears. It was a while before Masterji could get to see Ramu. Rupesh stood shifting his feet in silence, staring at the smirking men huddled over tea around the desk in the dark corridors of the jail. "Ramu beta," said Masterji, as he reached out his hand through the bars, "Why did you not send for us, why don't you look at us. Please say something, my boy? Slowly Ramu turned and as he stepped out of the shadows, Masterji gasped and stepped back in horror. Ramu's muffled cries rent the air as he pointed his crushed fingers to his tongue sliced in half and fell to the floor.

●●●

8

# Hatred is such a simple word

M r. Dutta walked in beaming a big, good morning smile at Shirley sitting on her desk outside his cabin. Shirley's halfhearted response did not go unnoticed. "Hatred is a very mild word for you," thought Shirley, as she followed the bulky form into the cabin. Silently she lay down the folder on his table and turned to leave. "Coffee please", boomed a voice behind her. "Indeed sir," said her voice, cursing him silently. "Who the hell do you think I am? No one has ever made such demands from me. I am not going to tolerate such impudence", she grumbled to herself as she poured out his coffee and placed it with a bang on his table.

Mr. Dutta looked up from his desk and wondered why Shirley was always in a foul mood. It was not his fault that Mr. Joseph had left the company. He knew Shirley had been with him for many years, but times change and people also move on. Besides he had given ample time to Shirley to get adjusted to his style of working. However, Shirley seemed to resent his every move and he did not know how long he was going to put up with this.

Shirley walked back to her desk and picked up the frame lying on her table and smiled at her photograph with

Mr. Joseph with his arm around her. How happy had they been working together. They understood each other perfectly and were a team for so many years. Each morning they would sit down together, schedule work for the day, discuss things over a cup of tea, and then she would go back to her desk and work would run like clockwork. No one dared to enter his cabin without letting her know, as she was the dragon they did not dare to confront and she knew it. She had protected him from all unwanted visitors, disgruntle staff, unnecessary interruptions. Then that fateful day, Mr. Joseph said he was resigning as he talked about his successor, a younger man who was the need of the hour. After all, he was getting old and it was too late for him to change, he said, "and besides between you and me, I don't want to go, but before they throw me out, I must make my way". Shirley stunned turned to stone as her eyes swelled with tears. She hated the management for doing this to him. Today it was him, tomorrow it could be her. A week later, Mr. Dutta, a young, bulky individual, had walked in reaching out to shake her hand. She hated him. After all, it was his fault that all this was happening.

Shirley put down the frame and sighed. She had tried and tried very hard to make Mr. Dutta understand that everything they had done was not a thing of the past to be set aside, but in no way was he willing to accept. He wanted changes, fast and within hours. Change the way we think, change the way we believe, change the way we do things, change the way we behave and the list was endless as Shirley's pen flew over the paper taking down the do's and don'ts in the inter department memo being dictated to her. He even ticked her off for her way she dressed asking her to shape up. He warned her that he would transfer her if she did not fall into line soon. His cabin door was open to anyone he instructed and soon people who could never dream of walking in unannounced, were walking past her, through the door smirking at her. The very people, to whom she was a demon then, were now looking past their noses at her with that 'you are no better than a doorman now' look. She felt humiliated and as each day passed she felt her self-esteem drop. She was fuming inside and she was not going to take it any more, but what could she do.

She walked into the cabin and sat down in front of him as he continued reading the document motioning her to wait. She watched him lick his finger and turn page after page. Yuk, she thought, how disgusting, and to think I have to turn those same pages after he corrects the same. She wished Mr. Joseph was sitting across her right now. If only, things were back to what they were earlier, but she knew it could never be. Then it happened. He put down the papers and began pointing out mistake after mistake in the document. "Why was he shouting?", thought Shirley, as her head began to spin till all she could hear was a buzz in her head. She sat there with her hands holding on tightly to the armrest. "I've got her exactly where I wanted her now", thought Mr. Dutta as he watched her squirm in the chair. It was his moment and he was not letting her off easy, as the tirade continued telling her how irresponsible she was. Her face turned ashen as she watched him smirking, nodding his head, and pounding the desk. Her heart snapped as she lost all control and her eyes narrowed in hatred as she walked out of the room.

The walls seemed to close in on her as she sat at her desk, hunched over, blank and bitter. That night she lay in her bed wondering why the world was crashing down on her. Lonely and alone in the world, her work place was her entire life. She cried hot tears onto her pillow curled up in bed hardly sleeping the whole night. In the morning, she dropped a bottle in her purse with a determined look on her face.

She tried hard to get those scary thoughts out of her head, as she sat there that morning at her desk. Slowly she got up, took a few deep breaths to calm herself and walked across to the smiling Stella as they shared a peaceful cup of coffee together. Stella, her one and only friend in the whole world she could count on. They shared a lot together at work, but she could not expect her to share a social life with her. After all Stella had two kids waiting at home.

Shirley placed the pile of mail in front of her and slowly started sorting it out, but her thoughts were wandering. Her hand involuntarily reaching into her bag as she took the bottle out of stared at it. No, she should not, she thought, and what was the use anyway. The problem was not going to go away. Today it was him tomorrow it could be a Mathew or a Sharma or anyone. She dropped the bottle back into her bag quickly as suddenly the door swung open. Mr. Dutta screamed a deadline at her, dropped the document on her table and he walked off away for a meeting. She stared at his determined form walking out of the office as she silently picked up the document and wondered how many more times it would need to be redone again. Seventy pages of the document would not take her long to re-do, she thought as she stared as his scrawled corrections and grimaced. Her heart was suddenly pounding hard, her mind was not with her and she could just not concentrate anymore as suddenly something snapped inside her.

Later that evening, Mr. Dutta walked in and noticed Shirley was not at her desk. "Damn the woman" he thought, "I bet she is gossiping with Stella about me." Calling Stella he barked, "send Shirley here, please", but Stella said that she was not feeling well and had left for the day. He cursed and picked up the document reading the pages, slowly licking his finger to turn the pages one by one. When all went quiet, Shirley unlocked herself out of the filing room. Slipping on a pair of gloves, she walked quietly over to the hunched figure pulled out the document from under him, replaced it with another

34

copy and dropped his head over it, patting him in a cursed goodbye. She walked out of the office and disappeared down the fire escape, out into the back street unseen by anyone.

The janitor found him next morning hunched over the document, dead as a doornail. No one knew when, how or what had happened, not even Shirley, who Stella vouched for saying she had left early that day. Poor man had died of a heart attack and he was so young, said everyone.

That evening at home, Shirley sat in her comfortable worn out armchair giggling nervously. Slowly the faint giggles broke out into a laughter, bursting forth like a rainy cloud. "Thank you Agatha Christie, or was it the brilliant Sherlock Homes", she said, "it was one of your brilliant murder mysteries that has freed me today." She had known he would lick each page of the document to turn the pages. All she had to do was lace it with an untraceable potion she had googled. She stared at the hundred of pieces of the torn document he had licked in the dustbin and dropped a match watching it burn and slowly flushed it down the toilet. As for the bottle of poison, she had already crushed it with a stone, and it would be lying somewhere in pieces strewn along the railway track where she had thrown it, standing on the footboard one piece at a time.

She had killed someone and still she felt nothing. No remorse, nothing at all. She was queen of the dark world now, confident and ready to take on anyone and anything. She was sure they would have to call Mr. Joseph back. After all who would step in at such short notice, but then that too now did not worry her anymore. She did not care anymore. Her demented eyes looked up at the night sky as she raised her head in a mock howl like a wolf crying at the moon and then stood silent and peaceful waiting for a new day.

•••

9

# The village pond

Amongst the cluster of mud-plastered huts shaded by a few trees, between the long stretch of green fields, the oxen carts creaked through the muddy broken roads, past women with covered faces, gracefully balancing water pots on their heads. The dust rose in a swirl and dropped with a whoosh, as the dirty dusty bus that passed through the village once each morning, whizzed past. The driver honked loudly as the hens ran helter skelter, diving out of the way of the big tyres skidding too close for comfort. The women turned away covering their faces with their saris till the dust settled, and the birds flew off squawking in fright. Silence came back to the road as the birds flew back to their perch singing a new merry tune nestling in the dark, interwoven branches.

A little distance away, fifteen mossy stone steps marching down led to the dark murky green water of the small village pond of the broken down fort, lay in silence. Dark green grassy patches surrounded the low broken down fort with its several wide entrances, pillars and dark interiors. Unpaved pathways meandered along its courtyard surrounding the village pond. Broken walls covered with moss stood peacefully, small temples and shrines sat in spaces under large shady trees. As dusk lay down its warm golden hands stretching across the village pond, Animandu watched the changing hues with bated breath calling out to the cattle, urging them to get out of the pond. It was getting dark and he knew, soon the village pond would turn violent. Strange voices would call out and tinkling feet would be heard running in the shadows of the fort. The shadows darkened and gathered over the pond, shaking and shivering as if in fear and the clouds covered the steps with dragon shapes reaching out into the water.

A small glow flickered from within the corridors as his heart started pounding. He prodded and poked the stubborn cattle out of the water. Slowly shaking their bulky bodies covered with water drops, glistening like diamonds in the setting sun, the cattle ploughed up the steps to the top laboriously clambering each step to the top. Animandu begged them to hurry it up prodding them when, suddenly the littlest calf broke away and ran into the dark corridors of the fort. Animandu stood rooted as if nailed to the ground watching it clamber up the broken steps and disappear. Oh no, he thought, he was not going to go after the calf. It was better to leave the calf there, than running through those deadly ghostly corridors searching for it.

Sevantika sat down in the shadows of the wall stroking the little calf with the largest brown eyes she had ever seen, as she watched Animandu struggling to get the cattle move down the path towards the village, fearfully looking back into the dark shadows. She smiled and gently pushed the calf urging it to run and join the herd, but the calf kept turning back, nuzzling and rubbing against her. The tinkling bells on her feet echoed in the empty fort, as she ran inside with the calf by her feet. She reached out behind the statue of the half broken dancing woman and pulled out the little tin box. The small lantern light flickered as she sat down in its warm glow counting her treasure, as she recalled the day she had opened it at home to find it empty. All her savings had gone. Her step-sister curled up in the cot, looked over her book, daring her to complain.

Sevantika's tears had dried up crying for those hours she had worked to save money for herself that day. She knew no one cared as she ran down the village square and soon found herself sitting on the steps of the pond watching the sun come down. She did not care if the ghosts of the fort took her away. In fact she wanted it to happen, as she got up and ran into the corridors, past the dusty carvings and broken down columns straight into the belly of the fort. Panting, she fell to the ground at the feet of the serene statue of the dancing woman lurking in the darkness. The shadows danced on the high cave walls with hundreds of broken statues almost alien. Her rasping breath echoed and then there was silence, as she slowly stood up peering in the darkness at the statues. They were beautiful she thought and suddenly she was not afraid. She twirled around running her hand over the carvings on the walls and began to dance like a courtesan in the court of a king, surrounded by statues with thick lips, big noses, slanted eyes, holding musical instruments staring at her as if alive. Round and round she danced, the bells on her feet tinkled as she cupped her hands over her mouth shouting to the silent statues, begging them to find her a loving husband. Faster and faster she ran around the corridors flicking her skirt, raising her hands in gay abandon. She climbed up higher to the top of fort's edge and stood precariously balancing on the highest column. As she raised her hands up to the sky drinking in the soothing rays of the moon howling like a wolf. Her heart felt unshackled and free and then she looked down to see running men and cattle streaking out of the village pond, screaming "Ghost!" pointing to her shadowy figure, her duppatta fluttering in the breeze above her head as if being pulled by the heavens above. Amused at the strange turn of fate, she laughed louder enjoying the moment, shaking her hands about in gay abandon, letting out shrill screams as she watched them run helter skelter in fear. She saluted the dark night, bowed to the trees and the silvery shinning moon, then waved to the glistening village pond below. Soon all was quiet, as she stood there peaceful and alone in the clear moonlight sky, queen of the fort and all she surveyed. Next morning, she heard the folk in the village talking in hushed whispers about their deadly encounter with the ghostly form atop the column of the haunted fort. Sevantika knew then that she had found the perfect place to keep her money away from the greedy hands of her uncle and his fat ugly daughter.

She sighed gently closed the box and placed it back in the crevice behind the statue with a fond smile, dusted off her long skirt, blew out the little lamp and sat down on the steps of the pond with the little calf trailing behind. She sat there in silence with her arm around the little calf, her feet twirling the cool water watching the shadow of the moon in the water as it jiggled and danced to the tune of the swirling water. "Aaah!" cried a voice. She jumped in fright as a hand rested on her shoulder. "So this is the ghostly shadow of the fort," said Animandu. Sevantika giggled as he sat down next to her. Thank God, that his father had insisted he bring back the calf, even if it meant him grappling the ghosts, thought Animandu. He had found the ghost and she had found a husband. Sevantika smiled shyly as they watched their shadows in the calm water of the village pond. The moon watched them indulgently, waited in silence for a while and then smiled brighter than before for them, as they burst into laughter.

●●●

# 10

# The forgotten night

The battle had gone on for months now, and the enemy's desperate attacks had not ceased. Gen. Walters knew soon his battalion would be out numbered, but it was getting impossible for them to break out. Ignoring all danger, he crawled around on his knees, thumping their backs and encouraging his men to continue to hold on to the line of fire. The last attack had been very intense and he knew now, that it was going to be impossible to save his post or the men. Gen. Walters bellowed an 'over and out', saluted a final goodbye to the post and then set about to destroy all the equipment. Signaling his men to retreat, he threw a grenade into the distance, in a final bid to save the day, and under the cover of its dust, watched the enemy disappear into the blackness. Silence filled the blackened sky, but it was not over. The enemy stepped out to a blaze of gunfire dropping some of his men like skittles, rising above the trenches like a huge black tidal wave with loud shouts of victory and captured them.

Months flew by, behind barbed wire of the enemy lines as they lay dazed, hungry, beaten and tortured. They had long given up hope of escape and in their weakened state they were sure they would never make it, even if they tried. Singing into the night to keep their sanity, was their only hope to stay alive. That too had become difficult as their parched throats begged for water. The enemy prodded them with guns and pouring water outside their cell teasing them as they reached out, drained, unable to touch it. Unshaven and tired faces stared at the grim General Walters, searching for answers. Each night one of them was dragged to the tent, their pitiful cries soon embracing death. That night he sold his soul to the enemy. In the quiet of the night, in exchange for his freedom, he signed the death warrants of the other men fighting in the cold snow capped mountains; the men, the friends, he had fought alongside. "Traitor, Traitor", rang his own voice in his head, as he lay down on the hard floor waiting for death which did not come. Morning came and the sun blinded their eyes as they were dragged into the waiting van, their heads pressed against the cracks, trying to see where they were going. The van threw them around inside for what seemed like eternity. Then all went silent as the noisy engine droned to a stop, the creaking door opened and the muzzle of the rifles nudged them out into the cold in the middle of nowhere and left them to freeze and die.

The bleak white horizon stretched in front of them in an endless nothingness. The cold breeze stung their cheeks as they ploughed through the knee-deep snow struggling to keep pace with life. Their souls egged them, on while their broken bodies cried out asking them to drop silently to a never ending sleep on God's white carpet. Their hands glued to their pockets, their rasped breath seemingly louder than a noisy plane as they marched on huddling together to keep warm as the harsh winds froze the very insides of their bodies. Their hands froze to stone as they tried to dig into the snow searching for shrubs to eat. They ploughed on praying and singing to keep their spirits high and as the barbed wires seemed to loom closer as they raised their hands for help. "Why had they not killed them? And why had death had not come to them?" he often wondered.

The war had continued but Gen. Walters was a changed man, shrunken and sullen. His deed buried in the depths of his soul never allowing him to sleep. Days passed staring at the flickering lights, clutching onto the remote, flipping it now and then, searching for those whom he gifted death to save himself. Then one fine day, the guns stopped booming, the sky cleared over the battle lines and weary soldiers marched homewards. His sunken and tearful eyes searched for his friends among the weary men waving into the camera. Morris, Johnson, Peterson were not amongst them. He had killed them by his betrayal. Life returned to normal, but not for the General as he walked each morning to the classroom to face the young enthusiastic recruits. They pressed him for war stories, oblivious of his tormented thoughts. How had they managed to survive? Who were the others? How did the others die? Did they give into the enemy? The questions were ripping out his soul and he could not take it anymore.

Then one day, Mrs. Morris came home to meet him and he sat in silence watching her arms hugging her tiny chest sobbing way into the late afternoon talking of her husband Morris, searching for answers. He sat there unable to move after she left. As the light began to fade, he stared at the wall decorated with photographs of his troupe, the line of medals, the photo of the fishing trip with Johnson, Morris and Peterson showing off their catch, and the other photographs of smiling soldiers all lined up neatly on the wall of his library.

His whole life flashed before him as he dropped down into the armchair, his weary eyes closed in resignation as he stroked the fire embers willing them to engulf his tormented soul. That night he did not sleep but sat hunched over his table writing late into the night. Morning came and the golden rays of the sun crept into the room, slowly resting on the lifeless form of the general. He lay there, dead in the armchair, a note on his chest under the silenced gun whispering the story of a traitor in a trail of smoke.

●●●

# 11

# From beyond the grave..

Amy stared out of the bus window staring at each passing village. Her three friends were busy singing and playing card games asking her to join in. She was more interested in the scenery and her favorite pastime of looking into the glass windows of the shops, as the bus wound its way through a village and out into the empty long roads once again through another village. As the bus wound its way through the dusty roads, Amy's darting eyes searched for names of the village on billboards and shop doors, her hand poised over the diary noting down the names as she read them. Green fields stretching into the far beyond, sunflowers reaching the skies, herds of scuttling cattle, farmers in the field, it was like a scene out of a movie. She was enjoying every bit of the ride. The river meandered through the plain running a race alongside the bus, with its waters bubbling over the stones splashing the banks with low hanging branches caressing its waters and the hut on a hillock. The bus soon sped into darkness and Sana's head rocked on her shoulder swaying to the tune of the bus wheels. Amy looked around at the silent faces deep in sleep with a smile. She pressed her head on the dark window pane and peered into the darkness cheering the moon on as it seemed to run alongside, shedding a warm silver light on the hillocks. Her eyes began to droop as the drone of the bus lulled her to sleep; only to be rudely awakened by Sana's head bobbing vigorously on her shoulder. The hot breeze blew in and out of the bus windows, as it hurtled down the winding stony road, rattling their bones, soon to screech to a halt for a break.

The four of them sat down on the broken table sipping on the hot tea enjoying the view. They backslapped each other, giggled at Raj's silly tales and ran down the little pathway to the small stream behind the shack. Kicking off their shoes, they sat down on the stones splashing water till the bus horn beckoned them to return.

A few hours later, there they were at Raj's village, standing outside his home. Her wrinkled and toothless face broke into a smile and Granny squealed in joy, clutching her grandson in a warm embrace. She looked at the girls, her eyes searching for the love of his life as both the girls stepped back with a nervous giggle wondering how they were going to stay in the almost broken down structure showing years of neglect on the mud walls. Inside the home it was another story. They entered into a whole new world with clean neat painted walls, decorated columns, high ceiling bedrooms with quaint ornaments and flower designs painted on the walls. Raj and Uday climbed to the top floor while the two girls took the room with huge windows, overlooking the outside courtyard. It was the cutest one they had seen with its large king size bed.

Amy sat down with a sigh on the huge parapet of the big brown wooden window looking out into the far horizon, her eyes drinking in the sheer magnificence of the hills stretching across the horizon like waves on the sea. A sudden chill ran up her spine as a shadow fell on her, but no one was near her. She chided herself for being scared and leaned out staring at the house far out there, on the hill. She felt that chill again, and her palms turned sweaty as she reached for the binoculars, peering into them. She fumbled with it and zoomed in on the dark blue one on the top floor and gasped. Sana found Amy slumped in a daze with the binoculars in her hand next to the window drenched in sweat. She lay on the bed mumbling incoherently as Granny gently wiped her forehead, stroking her arm. "I am just tired after the long bus drive. Don't worry I am fine" she consoled the friends. Amy, ashen faced turned her face away unable to explain the unexplainable. She was confused and wanted another look, but then maybe she was mistaken. After all she had not really slept well on the bus. Besides had her mother not always chided her that she was too much of a dreamer?

That night she willed herself not to look out of the window and chose to sleep the far in the corner on the couch in the room. Turning her back to the window, she drifted to sleep. A flash of thunder and Sana's deadly scream jerked her out of her sleep. Amy eyes stared in horror as she saw herself balancing precariously on the balcony. She jumped off into the waiting arms of the boys, dazed and unable to understand. The doctor came and they sat through the night trying to make sense of what was happening. Amy had no answers except that she knew what the house on the hill looked from inside. She described to her stunned friends, the pictures on the walls, the linen on the beds, the colours of the curtains, the room with the dark blue glass window, the flight of steps leading to it. She knew the number of steps too. They were thirty-four of them, dark green marble with a golden line in the centre, three landings and the tenth step with a chipped and broken corner. She knew about the pear tree with its branches falling all over the broken well filled with boulders in the inner courtyard, and she knew about the woman in the cold dark room below the steps. Then she began to cry as Granny rocked her gently.

They sat on the porch as Granny told the story of the house on the hill. "The house belonged to the richest man in the village. Grace was a devoted wife and a gentle woman who looked after the village folk like her own. Mary, the generous loving one and Jane the adventurous one, both unlike their mother, were like two wild birds soaring to touch the skies, as they ferried the river, danced in the village square and roamed the hills with their friends. Soon, they flew the nest and then one sad day Jane returned home a widow. She chose the room with the dark blue window and climbed up thirty four steps each day to the top, while her parents became recluses and stopped walking to the village square. Then came the day when the father died. Grace stood alone at the funeral as the villagers stared in silence. Jane refused to be there and Mary had been unable to come. "I still remember the pressure of Grace's hand in mine, her eyes seemed to want to tell me something" said Granny. A few months later, Mary had walked into the house with her two little sons darting up and down the steps sliding down the banister, racing each other. Days passed in happy laughter and cheer as they explored the village with their grandmother Grace and then it was time for them to leave.

It had been just two days since she had left and everyone was surprised to see George come back to the village looking for his wife. Mary had not returned home, he said. The boys had told their father that she had gotten off midway to return to the house saying she would be back in a few days, leaving them to continue with the servants. Jane was shocked, as everyone had seen her leave with the boys. The entire village had turned out to look for her but no one could find her and the police remain baffled till today. Grace collapsed that day and she now never steps out of the house", said Granny with a deep sigh. "It's been eight months since Mary died and no one knows how? The banquets and parties that had stopped when Mary had come to stay, now never seem to stop happening at the house. No one from the village goes there anymore, as some say Jane has turned bad. "I know what happened", whispered Amy staring across at the blue dark window as she continued to tell the shocking story.

"Mary watched indulgently as her boys drag her mother out to the courtyard laughing and playfully pulling at her skirt. Grace sat hugging the boys, her eyes filling with tears darting a scared look towards the house. Mary walked over and sat next to her. Hugging her daughter tightly, she gently slipped a note into one of the pockets, unknown to Mary. As they waved goodbye, Grace's heart almost missed a beat as her grandson pointed to his mother's pocket in a secret grin. She darted a frightened look at Jane but nothing seemed amiss as she walked back to the dark cold room below.

Mary dropped the letter onto her lap unable to believe what she read. Why had no one told her? Someone could have known. What was wrong with all of them? She stopped the car and told the servants to take the kids home, as turned and walked back to the house. Jane stared at the purposeful figure walking up the path. Mary barged in screaming, "how could you treat your mother like that, locking her in the cold dark room below the stairs, beating her, turning our home into a place of vice all for the love of the high life and money. Drinking and beating mother, and who is this man you are with these days," she said pointing at the man on top of the stairs.

The man dragged Grace into the cold room below the stairs and she stared in horror at the two sisters hitting, scratching and rolling all over the floor grabbing and tearing each other's hair out. Jane ran up the stairs as Mary sprinted after her screaming for her to stop. Grace turned on the man and bit the hand that held her, running after the girls. Jane pushed Mary to the ground and grabbed the candle stand perched on the ledge crashing it down hard on her sister's head. Grace screamed and fainted. When Grace woke up, she was lying in the cold dark room on her bed, her head heavy as lead. She ran up the stairs to Jane's room and stared at the floor and saw nothing amiss. The man had disappeared never to return. It was as if no one had been in that room. She was sure something had happened and she had heard them, then where was Mary?"

Amy paused as sweat ran down her brow. Granny touched her gently and asked, "Do you know why Mary was not found?" Amy nodded and continued, "Grace had been sedated for days and when she woke up it was as if nothing had happened. Jane showed no signs of any struggle, her long sleeved dresses hiding the tell tale marks. When George had come looking for his wife, Jane had feigned surprise and told him that Grace was unwell and it would not be wise to say anything till Mary was found".

Granny shook Amy and asked again "Do you know what happened to Mary, where is she?" "Come with me," said Amy as they walked down the long path, past the broken bridge to the house on the hill. Amy cringed as she reached the porch and then she took a deep breath. Her eyes turned cold and her face stony as she bellowed, "Jane, come down here". "Who is that", said a voice from the armchair near the fireplace. "Doctor... hello! Why are you all here? Mother is fine today and she is resting and Granny, what are you doing here? And who are these people?", asked Jane. "This is Amy and she knows what you did to Mary" said Granny with a stern look watching Jane's face turn ashen. "What utter rubbish. Who is this slip of a girl and what has she to do with Mary? The whole village knows Mary disappeared mysteriously." "No, she did not disappear," said Amy pointing towards the broken well with the branches of the pear tree falling all over it, "she is down there, under".

The boulders came off easily and a foul smell filled the air. Amy ran inside into the dingy room under the stairs and pulled Grace onto her feet clasping her bony frame, tears running down her eyes. The police handcuffed Jane and as they dragged her, she screamed at Amy, "who are you, who are you? How did you know?"

"It's me!! It's me... your sister Mary", she said, her soul slowly leaving Amy's body melting away into the night sky as Amy collapsed in the warm embrace of Grace's shocked arms.

●●●

## 12

# Frozen darkness

He looked over his shoulder nervously, as the thudding of feet continued to follow him. Picking up pace, he looked hard for an escape as the figure caught up with him. A flick of the raincoat and the bulky figure tipped his hat in a greeting and ran past him. Relieved, he gasped for breath and slowed down. Not a day had passed with him not imagining the worst, expecting the long hand of the revenge on his shoulder. He should have never agreed to be a part of the plan.

So many years had passed since that awful day, when he, Andre, stood on the deserted road, part of a group of men standing in the shadows huddled together. Music floated out of the large monstrous manor, as he bounded up the steps to the large wooden door into the ballroom his eyes searching for his prey. There she was, Francis, with a string of pearls around her swan-like neck, hair braided up with a peacock pin holding it up, soft curls caressing her neck, in her deep blue velvet dress swirling down to her ankles. She floated around, her soft tinkling laughter mingling with her husband's booming voice, hand in hand, as they stopped to talk to their guests. Then she turned, her eyes dimmed in fright, as she saw Andre walk slowly across towards them. Grabbing the folds of her dress, she practically dragged her husband into the sea of mankind that filled the hall and was lost to sight.

Francis, his love, or was he only using her? Andre never understood why he had been picked to have an affair with her. After all he was not at all good looking nor did he have a charming persona. He himself did not think too kindly of himself or his charm, but the group insisted he was the one and as planned, that day he deliberately bumped into her at the opera. Bending down to pick up the purse she dropped, their eyes locked and he had started to work his charm.

Here he was now closing in on her. He stood backing her pretending to talk to the big mustached gentleman making inane conversations, ears perked to pick up bits of conversation between the husband and wife. The Major was a traitor and they knew it. They had to get him to talk and now with Francis cornered, he knew he would get the information he wanted. He could see she was scared to see him there and now was time for him to get her to co-operate, after all her husband was too rich for her to throw away, and she needed his money for her lavish lifestyle. It was going great, he thought. Francis would soon be his too, so would all the money and the poor Major would hang for treason. It was going to work perfectly.

Andre followed Francis as she walked into the library and turned gracefully, removed the white gloves and beckoned him into her arms. The door opened with a bang and the lovers sprang apart gasping. The Major unleashed a volley of threats, slumping into the armchair near the fire place defeated, and then all hell broke loose. The Major begged for a fair trial but they would not hear of it and hung him from the gallows for treason. That night as Andre and Francis lay together, she talked unashamed of her deeds as the rest of the group hidden in the shadows listened.

Francis gloated that it was she who was actually "Deep Throat", the one that they had been gunning for and not the Major. She was the one running the network of delivering arms to the enemy lines. Her husband was her pawn and she used his name to cover her deadly deeds. The men melted out of the shadows and grabbed the shocked Francis, while Andre stood and watched his dream fade away. Days later, Francis stood composed in the court, her eyes not leaving his face and as the sentence was read out she hissed, "Andre, I will get you". That day Andre disappeared into the darkness of the night forever.

Then why now, after so many years, was he feeling this chill in his bones today? He was not within a hundred miles of her and except for Jacques and Richie, his aides in Operation Deep Throat no one knew where he was and they would not tell. He pulled his cloak closer and dragged his feet home. "Jane, I'm home, baby! Get me some coffee please" he called out as a voice hissed, "Jane baby is dead my darling and it's all your fault so go and get your own coffee". Andre ran into the room where Francis stood laughing over Jane's crumpled body lying lifeless on the cold floor, a stream of dark red blood oozing from under her. He dropped to the floor lifting his wife into his arms and rocked her like a baby crying "Why! Why her? She didn't do anything to you". "No darling, she did not, but her husband did", she said striking him with the smoking gun in her hand. "You cheated me. I was in love with you and I trusted you. We could have made a good life together but you used me, you scoundrel!" Her eyes narrowed with hatred screaming, "Here you are in some god forsaken place, crouching in fear, living your life. I told you I will get you. Did you think you could get away from me? No way! No! I have spent each and every moment in the hell hole waiting for this day." Andre cowered covering his head as she struck him over and over again. "I was only doing my job!" he said. "Only doing your job, only doing your job!" she ranted "So was I, till you came into my life and I fell in love. I wanted to tell you, make you understand. I was planning on telling you but you were using me to get to my husband! But then you never knew it was me, did you, until that night!!" she continued, "I was hoping you would understand and join me but no, you had to be the hero".

Andre tried to get up but she held the gun to his head, kicking him over and over again. He grabbed her leg and pushed her down, and as the gun went off into the ceiling, he frantically dragged himself away from her crazed outburst. Fumbling, he grabbed the gun in his desk as she slammed the drawer shut on his fingers and shot him in his leg as he screamed in pain. He knew she was just toying with him and he would never get away. It was now or never, he thought as he mustered all his strength and rammed into her. They fell in a heap on the rug next to Jane's lifeless body as they grappled with the gun. "How did you find me?" he breathed heavily grabbing the gun and pinning her down. Francis pulled his head down kissed him hard and laughed, as Jacques came out of the shadows holding the gun to his head. Jacques! Andre's eyes narrowed in hatred as he turned in one swift move and grabbed Jacques's leg bringing him down, the gun going off killing him instantly as he fell on it. Andre pivoted and smashed into Francis and slammed her face onto the hard cold floor and shot her in the shoulder. She slumped, screaming in pain as she lay there defeated. Andre dragged himself up and shouted into the phone. "This is Agent Andre. I've been attacked. Yes, attacked and my wife has been shot dead by a crazed woman and her accomplice. Yes, they are dead too. I shot them both", he said as he put down the receiver. Her eyes froze with hatred and he whispered in her ear, "Goodbye, my demented enchantress", and shot her between the eyes.

●●●

# 13

# Mixed-up death

Saturday night. She thought he was acting weird. They had made plans to go to the movies. Maybe he was upset at her for choosing a romantic movie. The conversation was stilted as she asked him what was wrong, but he remained quiet. Kruti placed her hand on his shoulder and said she loved him, but he was not amused. She tried to placate him and begged to tell her what was wrong. Then she knew. It was that air ticket he had wanted, to fly out to Kolkata. He wanted her father to allow him to fly in his name, after all father worked with the airlines and had enough free tickets entitled to him lying unused. Why waste them. He was not going anywhere anyway, then why was he not willing to let him use it? After all it was not like he was flying abroad, and who would question the name? They both had the same name R. Mathur. He was Ravi, her father Rajendra. Ravi grumbled, threw things at her, demanding that she speak to her father.

She went home swollen face and blackened eye and sobbed in her father's arms. Father was stunned blaming himself for the brute he had given his daughter to. The boy had been so well behaved, good-natured and his family was a big name in the business circles. The Mathurs were one of the most affluent families in his town. On the day of the wedding, they had entertained hundreds of guests, fed innumerable poor people and the whole area had been lit up. How could he have misjudged them? He stared down at his crying daughter stroking her hair as she pleaded with her father to give the ticket. He would kill her she said if it did not happen and she was scared to go back. Rubbish, said her father, he will do no such thing and pray, why was Raj insisting on a stupid thing like that? He could well afford to buy a ticket for himself. After all he too, was a very rich man himself. "I will buy you a ticket myself" offered father but Raj would hear none of it and as they walked out, he stole father's identity card unseen by them.

He stared at his wife as she stood there cowering. He did care for her but what could he do? After all, he had to get his father's dirty plan, going to get their company out of bankruptcy. Too much was involved, their reputation, their life style. The mafia was after them and it was not a small amount they owed. They had to get a great deal of money soon.

"It was all wrong," thought father "why is my son-in-law insisting on using my name? Something is just not right." A chill ran down his spine, as he grabbed his identity card and he followed their taxi silently, watched Kruti walk her husband into the airport. Her eyes widened in horror as she watched Raj slip the airline tag around his neck with his picture on it instead of her father's. He waved her off as he entered the terminal. Kruti stood there unable to move as a hand pulled her into the waiting car. She told her father about the forged identity pointing to the tag around his neck. Stunned, he looked at the tag around his neck wondering how Raj had managed to forge it. Nothing seemed to make sense. They drove in silence listening to the radio when suddenly all hell turned loose. Terrorists were on the plane and they had demands or they would blow it up they said. She somehow just knew it would be the flight her husband was on, and began to cry as she heard the flight number. Father screeched the car to a halt and turned around racing to the airport. They ran out of the car towards the departure area, but no one was allowed to go in, as her father dragged her to the other side of the airport looking out into the runway, as they watched the plane circle and land. They stood there for hours in fear as the never-ending saga began to unfold. Then it was all over, as a loud blast ripped the air as the plane burst into flames. She screamed and screamed as father dragged her to the car. The gravity of the situation sunk in fast. He was dead to the world. He was dead, not his son-in-law. It was his name on the list and he dare not get out there. He knew it had something to do with him but then why would Raj be on that plane, he wondered. Raj was dead and he was not? He dragged his crying daughter into the car and drove out into the darkness of the night, as the fire engines roared past. The city stood still, as the blare of the sirens screamed into the night. The words kept ringing in his head "I am dead to the world" to the drone of his daughter's weeping, but he was alive and what could he do now and where could he go. It was all wrong, but then his daughter too, was a widow. He dropped his daughter home but refused to come in telling her that he was going to be fine as he kissed her head and clasped her in his arms promising to call her in the morning. He dared not go home and he needed time to think. Father vanished to his farmhouse to think. He sat there, head in his hands trying to make sense. Later that night there was a knock on the door and father gasped in shock at the men standing at the door.

How was she going to explain her father's death to anyone? Why were her in-laws not crying for their son? Why were they so calmly sitting there watching the horrifying scene of the burning plane, weeping relatives crying for the loved ones as the fire engines roared past behind the reporter telling the story of a terrorist attack? Her blood froze as she watched unable to understand as her eyes slowly widened in shock at the photo of her father. Why was her father's face being shown on the television? The reporter's voice droned on and on as the telephone began to ring. She turned numb as she heard her father-in-law tell them the tale of a terrorist father, her father! She could not understand what was happening, but the panic attack would not go, but then who could she call? Why was father not calling her and where was he? She ran into her room and dialed her father's mobile but there was no sound at the other end. Tears ran down her face as the door flew open. Raj walked in tearing the boarding pass and throwing it at her face.

Her father never returned and she knew they had something to do with it. Soon she put the pieces together. R. Mathur, an employee, had walked into the terminal past security with the photo identity around his neck. Who knew the photo had nothing to do with the name and details on it. He had been on the plane and he was the bad guy, the one who had planned it all, the human bomb of a terrorist group. It had been easy for Raj. They had planned it to the last detail with the help of his terrorist friends and traitors at the departure lounge, sneaking her husband out of the tarmac after collecting the boarding pass. The terrorists, with their own agenda and demands had unleashed terror on the city using her father's name and identity, and her husband's agenda had been simply money. All he had to do next, was take them along to murder her father. He was dead to the world anyways and who would look for him, burnt to cinders at his own farmhouse in the darkness of the night. Her husband had got it all, her silence, her inheritance and their family was back in business. She knew now but she was trapped forever. She had no proof. And no one would believe her story.

●●●

# 14

# The folly of loving

Cathy stared at the calendar in her hand. It couldn't be true. It's such a nice and romantic phrase that says 'Love is blind', but it was too late to think about that now. She had made the mistake, and she was not sure whether he would stand by her. She walked into the room and stared at her mother lying frail in bed. Straightening the covers, she tucked her in lovingly and sat down to read to her mother. Mother's eyes drooped, as she waved her off that day gently, pushing her to get going. "You are going to be late again and Sam is not going to like it", she said. After all Sam had taken charge of their lives, and had it not been for him they would be sleeping hungry. Cathy ran down the street and jumped onto the moving bus as her hand gently clutched her stomach. She knew she should be more careful, but wasn't she just hoping her carelessness would wipe out her mistake? But then it never did work that way, did it?

Sam's piercing eyes seemed to go deep into her soul, as if reaching out to pull her heart out. Her hand clutched the pearls around her neck as she read to him. Her thoughts were not with him that day, as her mind wandered in the plains of despair, but she continued to read. Rosy, his old nurse, came in silently as she lay down the tray and fed him silently listening to her reading. Cathy was really beginning to get tired of sitting in front of a bed with the frail old body lying listlessly, listening to the drone of her voice. It was not, that she did not care. She loved him like a father, but she just wanted to get up and walk out forever. In the morning she came to read to her sick mother, and then it was Sam lying there waving his arms in annoyance each time her voice stopped. She stared at the book, not really reading it, for it was the hundredth time he was listening to the same words, as if studying for an exam. She knew the words by heart and she was sure he did too, as at every wrong word, he stopped to correct her. The tick tock of the clock, the sound of the fly as it zipped around her settling occasionally on the old man's arm, suddenly seemed to fill the room. She sat back and wrinkled her face waiting for it to settle so that she could zap it with the fly swatter, but it seemed to know what she was thinking, as it teased her buzzing around back and forth. Sam watched her eyes follow the fly with amusement daring her to hit it while it sat on his arm. Cathy's bated breath ebbed with a sigh of relief as the fly suddenly jetted out of the open window never to return. She lay down the book neatly on the table just the way he liked it, next to the glass of water close within his reach and walked out leaving Rosy to tuck the old man in.

Cathy walked into the study, settling down to work. The typewriter tipped and tapped as the words flew across the paper in a neat march left to right and again left to right in a boring tune. Soon it was done with, and she thankfully rose and walked into James' room. She smiled as she watched the handsome young son standing with his arm rested on the mantelpiece stroking the fire. Sam loved Cathy like a daughter, but James was another story. He hated his son for bringing shame to the family name by deserting his ranks. He had willed that he wanted nothing to do with his good for nothing son. Not that James cared, as after all, he was going to be rich one day and had never stepped into his father's bedroom ever since.

Margaret, the richest girl in town was already madly in love with him and wanted to marry him. Cathy was never going to be his wife, and he would not allow her get his father's wealth. She was pregnant and he knew that he had to get rid of her before it was too late. He was now sure that the time had come, as the old man had promised to leave it all to Cathy. He wanted Margret and the money.

They stood around him in silence, the old man lying there silent forever. James sat there, holding the old man's hand, his eyes swollen with tears no one seemed to believe. He told the inspector that his father had insisted on going to his manor on the hill. Maybe he knew death was close. The sharp eyes of the doctor did not miss Cathy's shocked face, her hand involuntarily stroking her stomach. James's face turned murderous as Cathy stood up to clasp his hand tenderly. "How dare you touch me, you slut, you gold digger. You were waiting for this day, weren't you?" he shouted shoving her aside.

A sudden sharp slap knocked James over as he stared into the haunting eyes of Rosy. "How dare you say things like that to Cathy?" she screamed, "you worthless man, you are no better!!!" She sank into the chair and continued "I am his mother", she said to the inspector, pointing to the shocked James. "Sam and I fell in love when I came into this house with his wife, Sarah as her maid. His wife never wanted children, but she knew a heir to the family was important, so she was more than happy with the arrangement. Sam moved us to his manor in the hills for months and we returned only after James was born. No one was any the wiser. But James! He was never the son Sam hoped for. He had shamed him, and he used me

61

when Sarah died telling him the secret. I could not ask Sam for money and could not go on stealing money for him too, as Sam was beginning to suspect. Then Cathy came into his life, and Sam told me he had found the love he had always wanted from a child. One day, I found Cathy crying in the kitchen and she told me she was carrying James' child, and I promised to stand by her. When I told Sam that day that he was becoming a grandfather, tears of joy roll down his eyes as he clasped my hand telling me how happy he was. James had made him a happy man after all. I too was content that my son had Cathy and he would no more need to worry about money.

Then last evening, my drunken son told me his plan. He was going to take Sam to their house on the hills and there he would get rid of Sam before he changed his will. The foggy hills had many accidental tales to tell and a car rolling down the hill was not unknown to the darkness. Cathy had no proof that the child was his, and he did not care for her. I could not let that happen and threatened to tell Cathy. James dragged me with him and threw his father on the back seat like a sack of potatoes and then pushed me in at gunpoint. Up the dark paths to the manor on the hill, the car kept twisting and turning as Sam's frail body racked in pain, his eyes imploring me for help. I held on to him as hard as I could, begging James to stop, but was unable to do anything, and before I knew it Sam's eyes turned into stone as I watched life leave his body. James was thrilled with the turn of events as he turned the car around straight to the house. I could do nothing except watch him. He laid his dead father back on his bed and then phoned the doctor. But you know James, he had already changed his will and you are not in it. Cathy is, but I decided not to say anything. So even if you had gotten out of this mess, you would have lost everything anyway by choosing Margret over her".

James grabbed Rosy by the neck in rage, "He changed his will and you never told me". Rosy shrugged him off, and soon the room turned silent as the inspector rose and walked over to James. James stood there in silence staring at the handcuffs circling his wrists. "Why did you not tell him that Sam had changed the will, Rosy?" asked Cathy clasping Rosy in her arms. "I did not have a chance. Sam was dying in my arms and I knew it was too late to save him", she cried. The two women cried for the man they loved. Morning came, and Cathy, the new lady of the manor, tucked her mother in Sam's bed with a smile and gently kissed her forehead.

●●●

# 15

# The whispering night

Laila broke into a cold sweat. It was that voice again, she told mother. Mother did not believe her, but she heard it every night. The groaning of someone in anguish and despair, close to her ear, and definitely on the pillow next to her. The soft breeze caressing her forehead, as if someone was patting her to sleep. The voice whispered softly into her ear. The window opened and closed as if someone was walking through it. She never dared to open her eyes or turn in her bed till she heard the window slam, and then she would jump out of bed, wincing as her feet touched the cold stony floor, fearfully moving closer to the window to stare out into the night. She had never seen anything till today, but now she was sure she saw shadows moving in the dark. The shadows floated down the ugly pathway that forked out into the woods, spreading its tentacles across everything in its path, past the cemetery to its left, and the shambled greenhouse leading to the big iron gate. The autumn leaves swirled up, and dropping dead weight onto the cobbled stones, again rising and falling as the wind whistled through. She stood silently watching the leaves dance around the shadows as they disappeared into the thick woods. Her blood froze as she strained her eyes to peer into the thickness of the trees for another look. She was not sure but it seemed the shadows were looking right back at her with their hands spread as if asking her to embrace them. Her heart fluttered as she stepped back and drew the curtains in one swift move and jumped into bed covering her head.

If only she could understand what they were whispering. It never stopped. "Leave me alone," she screamed throwing her pillow at the window as mother rushed in. "Hush Hush, nothing is there and no one is in the room", she said, as she rocked her in her arms. Laila cowered into her mother's arms her eyes glazed in fear. "They talk to me mother, but I don't know what they are saying. Why are they tormenting me every night? What do they want? Why are they not doing something?" she cried.

Mother rocked her late into the night occasionally stealing a look at the closed curtains. The clock struck three and soon Laila's eyes drooped and as she snuggled into the pillows, Mother gave a sigh of relief tucked her in and closed the door. The house was too huge, and what had possessed her to rent it, she just did not know. Maybe it was the huge rooms, the grand bedposts, the winding stairway to the huge hallway or maybe the beautiful dome with its colored glass painting. Most definitely, the row of beautiful mirrors lined up along the long corridors, she thought. She loved the way the light streamed in from the dome onto the mirrors. She never passed the mirrors without stopping to straighten her hair and as she stood there smiling and looking at her reflection in the mirror, she gasped. She saw shadows behind her in the reflection. Now she was beginning to see things too.

Admonishing and smiling to herself she walked down the long corridor and sat down in the kitchen pouring her a pot cup of tea. Soon it would be daylight and she decided she was going to take Laila to the parish. Maybe Father John would be able to help. She sighed remembering how the old man in the café had warned her not to rent the house. "It's an evil place", he had said, "very unsafe for two women in that big house. No one has ever lived there long enough. It won't be long before you too will see things. It has a past. Beware the autumn moon". She had not believed a word of what he had said, after all, she was an army man's widow, but now three weeks had passed and Laila had not slept a night without screaming.

The old man at the café had warned her every time they met and maybe she should have listened. She walked to the café and over a cup of tea, he told her the story. A little girl living there had been axed to death by the gardener because she saw what she should not have seen. The deranged father of the girl had avenged her death by shooting his adulterous wife and her lover, the gardener. They said the neighbours had found him talking to the body, with his two year old son crying and clasped to his chest. He believed his daughter would come back from the dead one day. They locked him away for murder and when he returned, they shut themselves up in the outhouse. The benevolent villagers fed and looked after them for many years but one day the father died a lonely death waiting for his daughter to come home. That night, his son crawled into his father's grave and was found dead in his father's arms. Many came to stay but strange voices scared them away and the house remained closed for many years. "Be warned", said the man at the café, "Your daughter is in more danger than anyone has been before. She is Laila, and that's what the little girl was called too. Today is the day she died. The autumn moon will rise at midnight so get out of there before that". Mother stood up with a nervous giggle as she refused the man's offer to shift to the café that night.

She got up with a sigh as the clock struck eleven and as she climbed up the stairs to her room, she could not resist another look at the mirror. She stopped and peered closer at her reflection to straighten her hair and gasped as the reflection she saw was not her own. A shadow, nothing but a shadow of a man with a boy clasped to his chest stared back at her. She stood rooted disbelievingly, staring, as it whispered, "The autumn moon will rise soon. My daughter, Laila, has come home, she will be mine tonight".

She stepped back in horror running up the stairs two at a time. Mother grabbed the sleepy Laila saying over and over again "I am sorry baby! I should have believed you. I am sorry" as she sprinted down the stairway. "Stop, stop. Don't leave the house Mother they can't hurt us here. Not the woods, not the woods, they live there" " screamed Laila, but Mother would not listen. "Run Laila, run baby! We have to run" she screamed dragging her into the courtyard, as the heavens burst into winds of hell whipping up the leaves into a storm. The shadows that rose in the darkness screeched, "Come back Laila, come back Laila, my daughter, we won't let you leave. The autumn moon will rise soon and you will be ours", as their shadows twirled around them.

"Run towards the lights in the courtyard, Mother, run and let's get out of shadows. They won't be able to hurt us in the light", Laila said, as she dragged her mother under the courtyard lights. They sat down under the soft glow of the lights clutching each other, as the shadows circled calling out to her to come into the darkness of the woods. "Leave the light and come here Laila", cried the shadows, "please come to us". The autumn moon that rose slowly in the sky, stared down disdainfully at the shadows circling around them.

"Go away", screamed Laila, "I am not your daughter". "You are... you are" hissed the shadows, "Come to us please, we need you, we love you," they said. She closed her ears and grabbed mother tight, as mother stared at the rising silvery moon willing it to fade into daylight. The two shadows lurked around the edge of the dark woods calling out to her, "come to us, baby, come into the woods, we've been waiting a long time for you, come to us before the autumn moon fades".

The hands of the watch moved to three and Mother stared at it, as if willing time to move faster. They stared at the iron gates looming ahead of the dark pathway without lights wondering whether they would be able to reach there if they ran. Even if they did, would they be able to pull open the heavy gate in time? The moon high in the sky smiled wickedly as the woods glistened in its light. "Wait till its morning, baby, we are safe here," said Mother, 'It's almost four now and we will be safe soon, the sun is almost up. They will go away". The shadows wrapped themselves around the gate snarling flying back and forth into the darkness of the pathway to the courtyard willing them to come out and run. It seemed to them like the sun was taking its time to rise that morning, when suddenly, the lights of the courtyard began to close one by one. Why was Ramu switching the lights off so early this morning? "It's only four o'clock, you idiot. It's still dark", mother screamed and waving to the servant in the far distance, blissfully unaware of the terror he was unleashing on them. "Why did I come out of the manor and walk you straight into their arms, Laila? I should have listened to you!" cried mother as the courtyard turned dark with each light blinking shut. They had nowhere to go but to make a dash for the gate. The menacing shadows rose out of the dark woods, when suddenly the iron gates swung open and out of the dawn, a horse cart whipped its way through the shadows wrapped around the iron gates. The shadows scratched the old man from the café as he whipped the horses towards the two women. They clambered on, as the horses galloped down the pathway to escape. The shadows grabbed Mother and pulled her off the cart as the old man screeched the horses to a halt.

Laila jumped off the cart and raced after them as the shadows disappeared into the dark woods, wrapping themselves around her mother, lifting her up into the sky threatening to drop her, as she screamed in pain. "You won't get me if you hurt her! Leave her alone and come get me", Laila screamed. The shadows turned and dropped her mother to the ground. Dark and scary, they turned, whipping up a frenzy to get to Laila who began running away from them. "Get out of the woods, Laila. Run to the gates, run into the sunlight", screamed the old man. Laila knew she had to get out of the dark woods to the gate and as she sprinted towards it, she prayed for the sun to rise faster. She ran as fast as she could, zigzagging around the tree trunks but it was too late. The shadows grabbed her leg pulling her back into the dark woods into their dark embrace. As they dragged her through the woods, the first rays of the sun pushed their way through the trees only to get stuck among the thick branches. She heard the other shadows in the woods lashing around amidst the dark trees venturing out of the woods and fading into wisps as slowly the sun-rays pushed their way harder through the branches. Laila closed her eyes waiting for the end to come as they whispered lovingly in her ears, but nothing seemed to be happening to her. The shadows made feeble attempts to hold onto her and soon they dropped her at foot of the tree, where she lay struggling for her breath. "So many autumn moons have come and gone but you never came. Don't go Laila please", pleaded the shadows struggling desperately to reach her. Laila stood up safe in the arms of her mother as the dying shadows caressed her cheek one last time and sobbed, "We will be back for you, my dear. You will have to come home, my daughter. You will come back, Laila".

●●●

# 16

# Help us please

The mobile rang and he sleepily reached across to pick it up. "Damn you, Sushmita, why do you always call when I am half asleep? Hello," he said, but the call got disconnected so he rolled on his back and went back to sleep. On his way to work suddenly he remembered he should have called her back. Pulling out his mobile, he quickly called the number and banged it down in frustration as the voice crooned, "Your call is on hold" for the tenth time. Engrossed in work, he did not realize how the time had flown. He tried again. This time it crooned, "this number does not exist". "What the hell. Where are you Sushmita?" he grumbled as he reached out to call again the residence number, but there was no answer. Maybe her plans had changed, maybe she was not back from the tour.

Sushmita sat leaning her head against the car window, the soft breeze caressing her hair. She should have called him again before leaving, she thought staring at the mobile flickering a low battery sign. She looked at her watch, as it shone in the dark. Never mind, she thought, it would only take a few hours to reach anyway, as she typed out a message to him instead. As her hair tousled around her face, she wound up the window and asked the driver to switch on the air conditioner and was soon fast asleep in the cool comfort of the car. A sudden jerk broke her sleep and she sat up just in time to see the driver swerve and miss the couple crossing the road, fumbling on the road in fright. The car rammed into the sandbank at the edge of the road, as Sushmita watched the couple and the driver argue while she sat there watching, not wanting to interfere. The young lady stood there dressed in a red floral outfit, neatly tied hair with a hint of sindoor in its parting, gold bangles jingling in her hand, the other hand holding on to the very wobbly man in his black suit and tie. Certainly not from around here and the man is definitely drunk, she thought. Besides there had been no accident, no one was hurt and definitely it was her car that hit the sand.

"Take us to the hospital please", she said. Sushmita watched the lady lovingly help the man into the front seat and then get in next to her with smile of thanks. "May I use the phone?" she asked, but Sushmita moved it away saying the battery was low and she had a long way to go. "You can have my number though," she offered knowing full well that they wouldn't be able to call her later. Anyway, once she dropped them at the hospital they would not need to keep in touch. In no time they had reached the hospital and as they got out the lady turned her face pressed into the window, her grateful eyes seemed to bore into Sushmita's heart as she mumbled a thanks. "Hmmm, he is definitely drunk" thought Sushmita, as she watched the couple climb the hospital steps, as the car moved away.

Sushmita sat back pulling her feet under her and reached for the magazine. The car had not gone far when it suddenly stopped again with a loud crunch. Looking up from her magazine, Sushmita saw the ashen face of the driver staring at the two figures standing on the road, and as she turned to look, her blood curled. There she was again pulling the wobbly man across the road. She cringed into the seat as the lady walked towards the car window motioning for the mobile lying next to Sushmita on the seat. The rolled up glass window seemed to melt as Sushmita stared unbelievingly. "Sorry I can't help you. Driver, move, move" she said urging the driver to hit the accelerator. Sushmita stared out of the back windscreen watching the receding figures on the road.

"How can it be possible", thought Sushmita, as she motioned the driver towards the roadside café. Totally drained staring at the watch in her hand showing way past eleven, she turned the mobile around in her hand staring at its now dead screen and dropped it back into her purse with a sigh. The hot cup of coffee soothing her nerves, she watched the driver telling his story with flourish to the people with him on the next table. As she made herself comfortable in the car, the driver turned and said "Memsab! I have heard the most awful story. The other drivers tell me that three years ago a young newly married couple had been driving down this road when their car overturned and rolled off the road into the hill below, a little away from where we saw them. The husband broke his back in the crash and as he lay on the floor of the upturned car moaning, his wife ran out onto the highway screaming for help. No one seemed to see her or hear her as she ran towards the crowd that stopped to stare at the crash. She begged them to give her their mobile so that she could call for help, to call her family, but they seemed to look through her. That night the police took the bodies away, the husband was found dead on the floor of the car while the wife lay thrown out of the car, her body hanging from the tree. The villagers who saw their bodies say that every year on that deadly night of their death, she is seen on the road, holding the hand of her husband with his broken back, trying to stop cars asking for a mobile to call home for help. Today was the day they died!!".

Sushmita shivered and shook in fright as her mobile ring. How could it ring? Her phone was dead long ago. She pulled out the mobile from her purse and stared at the blank screen of her mobile. It continued to ring and as she raised it to her ear, she heard a woman say "You dropped us at the hospital and gave us your number, remember? Please call our family. Help us please! Help us please!".

•••

17

# Terror unleashed

He stood in the street watching the terror unfurl before him. He saw people running helter-skelter, crying and dragging each other across the street, with its high rising buildings. The windows shut tight in fear. The beautiful flower market with its marigolds, lilies, roses and garlands lay crushed to a deep red amongst the dead. He wondered whether this was Mumbai, the city of dreams that he dreamt of. They said the city that never sleeps, but was it ever going to sleep again? No, he knew it would not for some time now. He was sure and he was the one responsible. Dispassionate and glazed, his eyes did not waver as he ran into the street to grab the nearest person out of the ripped bus. The hands holding on to him hard, and the moaning close to his ear, did not affect him as he pulled her to the corner of the road into the waiting arms of the others. For the next two hours all he did was drag and pull, his aching arms covered with blood that did not seem unusual. "Bless you," said the old man and his son as he helped them bandage their wounds sitting on the stairs of a shop baring its soul, completely destroyed and ripped open. He watched the policemen running around pushing people away from the flaming cars, cordoning off every corner of the street.

The golden colours of the hot flames rose to the sky melting into the orange setting sky, frowning upon the mayhem below, as the roads covered with blood bore witness to the carnage. He helped the injured and got into the van with them and as they moved off the street, his lips curled to a smile.

He had done it and they were going to be pleased. No one could ever have guessed why or what had hit them, as there were no traces to prove anything and that, they had made sure of. Besides who would ever imagine that this blood covered individual who was so helpful was the one who was responsible for the bombing. The silence in the van broke as the occupants slowly broke out of their shocked stupor and cursed the people responsible. He did not participate in the conversation, but stood there looking at the hatred on the pained faces. Slowly his face turning ashen, as the harsh words sank into the deep dead crevices of his heart. He felt the world spinning around and when he awoke there he was lying on the seat of the van. Someone was pouring a trickle of water down his throat. "No," screamed his mind, "I don't deserve this". He struggled to his feet as the men around him helped him up with words of encouragement and patted his back in thanks for his help on the streets. He could not look into their eyes, he had to get away. What was happening to him? This was not the way it was to be. The warm touch of hands on his body helping him up seemed to melt the very core of his being. Tears, it could not be, he thought; it has to be the wind on his perspiring face. "Stop the van! Stop! Please. I want to get off", he screamed, as he jumped out and ran mindlessly into the ravaged street of running feet till he could run no more, and collapsed on the curb his body racked with sobs.

He sat there staring at the mayhem, his mind floating back to that fateful day he met 'The Man'. Harassing the greedy landlord had become a routine for them. Each morning the boys would meet under the peepal tree and decide what next, and soon they would be hiding in the bushes near his mansion. That day, the stones and reeds set on fire rained down hard on the red tiled roof making deafening sound. Soon the reeds burnt the house down. They hid in the bushes enjoying the chaos they had reigned upon the landlord huddling with his family trying to escape the flying flames leaping out of the windows slowly burning all they owned to cinders.

Drunk with power, they sat far in the hills looking down on the village as 'The Man' began telling stories of the life in the city. Slowly and surely the young men huddled around the fire were soon more ignited than the fire they sat around. The Man promised them money more than they would ever get in a lifetime living in the village. He had always dreamed of Mumbai and now he had a way to get there and that too all on a platter. That night he lay awake, convincing himself that it was just a job and if he did not do it, someone else would do it and someone else would make the money. They had always called him the black sheep in the family, a leech who just ate and slept and never worked a day of his life. Now it was time to prove to them that he too could make money and that too lots of it. He was going to return with so much of it that they would all be running after him. It was going to be a while before he would ever see the village streets again and soon the train chugged way into the darkness towards the city. The first time he held out his hand for the money, he realized there was no backing out.

He had killed so many innocent people in the past, then why was he hurting today. Maybe his sins were catching up with him, or maybe the fire had died inside him or maybe he was just not thinking straight today. Nothing seemed to make sense, but he somehow knew he could take no more. It was never going to be the same again that, he knew for sure. Slowly he dragged himself up and walked out into the noisy streets trying to avoid the running feet, screaming vans and blaring horns. People were running and they did not seem to know where they were going. The streets were burning and it was as if everybody had gone mad. He knew he had started it. He slunk into the side streets, hiding in the shadows and stopped to take a breath when a sudden searing pain shot through his body. He looked up in horror at the hand holding a knife retreat into the madness, as life began flowing out of his body. They did not need him anymore. He knew now that his work was done. He had to die. The voices around him began to fade, his body floating and falling to the ground gasping in pain, as he found himself being lifted into an ambulance. His breath came in short rasps, eyes clouded and his body trembled. He lay there dying amongst the injured and dead he was responsible for; just another unclaimed body that no one would know.

●●●

# 18

# The ghostly manor

The manor had been empty for years, and only ghosts seemed to linger in the abandoned house. The caretaker sat at the large wooden gate, day after day still as death, his frozen eyes staring at the line of children cycling the long road to the orphanage up the hill. The three boys lagged behind to take a better look peering at the high moss covered windows hoping to see something. May be the two missing girls?

Rosy and Amy were best friends. The boys had seen them inseparable, like two peas in a pod. They were always together and seemed happy at the orphanage. Why would they just disappear from the orphanage? They were told the girls had run away, but they were sure that was not true. The boys had seen them that morning stopping to pick flowers near the gate of the manor. Maybe they should have waited for the girls. Maybe the ghosts of the manor had taken them away that day. Something was not right, they were sure.

They had to see if there were really ghosts in the house. They had to find Amy and Rosy. The boys laughed as they looked up in the sky. It was a full moon night. Perfect night to catch ghosts, they thought as they pedaled into the dark night towards the manor, the light of their cycles showing the way. The lonely stool stood forlorn at the wooden gate of the manor, as they waited for the caretaker, but he did not come! They waited with bated breath and wondered where he would be. Hiding their cycles behind the bushes the boys slowly crept over the wall and jumped into the dark manor grounds. The towers rose into the sky with its dark iron barred windows, as the green dark vines clung to the walls spreading like a skeleton's palm green, with ghoulish moss hanging precariously like blood oozing from a wound. The grass beneath their feet crackled sucking in the soles of their shoes as they squished onto the barren pathway motioning each other to silence. Running into the entrance to the tower was easy, but the darkness of the spiral staircase was too black and scary, daring them to take that first step.

The boys blinked in the darkness peering up the huge stone steps and started climbing. Their dark shadows followed them on the walls of the twisted stairways overtaking them sometimes and falling back, as if pulling the boys back. The boys froze in fright and giggled nervously at their shadows playing games with them as they climbed higher and higher, the light in the windows glistening in the rising moon. Clutching at the damp mossy walls, the boys clambered up the daunting dark high steps panting to a stop at the barred dirty window gasping for breath to suck in the cold night air. "One hundred and five", gasped one of them plonking down on the cold stair for a breather. The old iron door with its huge hinges loomed a few steps up. It creaked as they clenched their teeth pushing it open like swing on a rope.

There he was, pouring over books spread all over the large wooden engraved table in the darkness of the long room. On another large wooden table in the middle of the room, lay Amy tied down, silent as death. The moonbeam piercing down through a small hole in the roof onto her pale frozen face. Strange unexplainable bubbling noises echoed in the dead of the night as he shuffled around, raising his hands holding a knife to the sky mumbling and shaking in frenzy. On the floor sat a big black cat dark as the night with golden eyes, snarling and hissing at them as the boys sprung back not daring to breathe, melting into the wall. The caretaker heaved himself off the wooden table and raised a knife muttering, "Bow to the king, oh silvery moon. It is time". They had to do something. As the caretaker lifted the knife to stick it into Amy's body, the boys rushed out of hiding, screaming like banshees. He dropped the knife in fright and grabbed them one by one throwing them across the floor like skittles across the dark cold stone floor into the small cell. As they lay there gasping for breath, Rosy stared back at them, hairs strewn across her face and shouted, "He will kill Amy and I'm going to be next if his potion doesn't work. Don't let him get away. Untie me. Quick, let's get him now before he closes the door on us." As if struck by lightning all at once, they rammed into the caretaker and landed with a thud on him. Rosy untied Amy as the boys began to throw things at him. Books, pots and pans flew all over the place as they continued to throw whatever they could grab and closed the door on him. Running down the steps was the hardest thing ever, but the darkness of the stairs did not seem to matter any more. They jumped down the stairs two steps at a time, falling over each other. They knew the door would not hold the grappling hands of the caretaker.

Darting out of the manor, they grabbed their cycles and raced out into the street. A car flew out in front of them. The caretaker's grim face turned the car around and rammed into them. Swerving and braking they veered past the car and soon were racing with the car looming behind them for a few bends and then appearing in front for some. They thought they knew the road up the hill to the orphanage like the back of their hand but it was dark and the roads seemed so unfamiliar in the moonlight. Their hands were shaking and feet pedaling to save their lives. Amy and Rosy hung on to the handlebars as they pedaled out of the way from crunching wheels of the car swerving so close. Pedaling furiously huffing up the slopes as fast as they could. "Watch out for that bend" screamed Amy but it was too late. Their cycles got tangled together into a mad roll. It all happened so fast that before they knew it, they were rolling downhill the side of the road grasping desperately at the grass tuffs on the way down with their cycles turning and twisting in the air falling down with them. A deafening silence suddenly filled the air as they clutched onto the branches hiding in the shadows with bated breath and watched the cycles fall with a crash on the road below. The car engine droned to a silence, the rustling of his feet dropped pebbles onto their heads, as they hid there unseen by him. They waited, not daring to breathe until the deadly silence was broken by the drone of the car as it swerved down the hill towards the falling cycles.

They pulled themselves up and dropped down, wide-eyed and shivering as the whirr of the car receded far into the night and out of sight. Picking themselves up, they ran as fast as they could to the warmth of the orphanage, straight into the worried arms of the headmaster. The caretaker confessed his crime to spells and black magic! "It's all in the books. I had the potion and magic to become immortal. I would have been king of the world. I was meant to be a king this full moon night" he ranted as he was dragged away, "all I needed was a young girl's blood."

●●●

81

## 19

# It had to be, for better or worse

Black as night, darkness all around, then why is the colour of the stick white, he wondered. Or so they said it was. He could not see it partly anyway and wondered what others could see when they saw a white stick. "At least I still do have some vision but as each day goes by its becoming worse," he talked to himself, as he walked along. He tapped along the road, a rhythmic tune to the sounds of the world, and his heart started to beat faster as he found his way to the station. Her warm hand clasped his forearm sending a warm feeling of safety down his spine as his mouth curled to a smile. Sam had met her just the other day at the station. Trying to get into the train, his cane got there before he did. So had a young lady with an armful of packages. She had got tangled up with his cane and packages went everywhere.

He had slipped and fallen to his knees, her soft voice urging him up holding his hand. They talked all the way and when it was time to part, her soft voice asked him if she could be is companion every day. Sam's eyes moistened as tears rained down his crinkled disfigured skin. Did she not feel horrified looking into his ugly face? He wondered what she looked like. All he could see was a blur of a pretty face. She had to be young, her voice certainly sounded young and the touch definitely felt so. Maria, what a lovely name.

Every day they would meet at the corner and as they made their way towards the station together, she would paint a picture of things around them. The fat woman in the green sari dragging her little skinny boy along the road, the school children with orange ice-creams dripping down their hands, the rickshawalla wiping the sweat off his brow waiting at the corner, the cobbler at the corner of the street tapping away at a shoe. The blurs he could see were complete pictures now as he saw the world through her eyes. Sometimes they stopped to sit at the park bench and share a packet of groundnuts in silence.

He now knew she worked at a music store not far from his own telephone booth. Sometime during the day she would walk across and ask him how he was doing, share lunch and then in the evening she would be back holding his hand. He knew he was falling in love with her, but he knew he could never ever tell her. She would leave him for sure if she knew. He wondered what she felt.

"You know I used to dread having to make a train journey on my own from home to the booth", he told her one day as they walked together, "I had no idea what was happening and no one would tell me! Even when stations were announced, I could hardly hear over the noise in the compartments and so I'd end up having to count every stop. I have to change trains, and sometimes it was complete disaster because often there is little time between connections and everyone is forever in a hurry, pushing me around. As for those ever large gaps between the train and the platform! It's just as tricky as can be for me. Many times, I am deep in thought and have drifted off onto the road. Once I almost got hit by the cars passing by on the way to the station." She laughed, "I too have a problem like you, I have just two fingers on my left hand and I know what its like to be getting on and off trains and buses." He gasped as he reached out to touch her fingers for the first time. 'So you see," she said," both of us have been troubled by life. I have no family what about you?"

"I was not born blind, you know" he said, "I was only fifteen when I was pushed off the tree by a friend. I fell ten feet onto a heap of burning grass below then the sights started to fade, slowly and steadily and I could do nothing to stop it. The taller I grew, the bigger the cane became. Then one day, you know I climbed up the tree again. I felt like I could do everything that day, but I will never forgive my friend, you know. I never will, and though I still can see things blurred, it's not enough to get by you know. I have learned to survive". They sat there in silence and then he reached out to see if she was still there. "I did not know and that's very sad, you know, because forgiveness is important in life. I thought you were a compassionate man but you have so much hatred in you. That means you probably don't need me either, so I'm leaving you", she said and let go of his arm.

"No, no, Maria, that's not what I meant" he said, watching her shadowy figure disappear in a blur. He grabbed his stick running after her. "Why did I ever say something like that", he thought as he tried to make pictures of the blurs in front of him searching for her. Then the loudest bang he had ever heard with a loud scream that sounded so familiar filled the air. "No, no" he screamed as he tried to get past the running feet, not knowing which direction to turn. Grabbing the arm closest to him, his fears turned to reality. He pleaded to be taken to her and dropped down near her.

Sam touched her face gently as she lay there on the hospital bed. He was responsible for her accident, he knew it. Days passed before she came out of her coma, her screams renting the air, "Not my leg, not my leg!" She touched the leg feeling the hard iron rod in her thigh. Maria grabbed his arm and sobbed as he ran a hand over her head. That day, they cried for their handicap, wondering at the cruelty of fate. They sat in silence as the sounds of night turned to dawn.

"Forgive me, Maria, for I hurt your feelings. The accident would not have happened had I not been so foolish and self centered", he said, holding her hand. "I was hurt for a long time you know. I had no one in my life before and so I guess I really did not understand." "No, she said, "I deserve this, it's my punishment. First it was my hand and now my leg. It's you who needs to forgive me. It's my fault. I should have never, never pushed you off that tree. I lost my fingers that day trying to grab you as you fell. We were forced to leave town because of my injury, but I never stopped thinking of you. You know, I used to close my eyes and walk around the house just to feel your pain. My parents tried to make me forget you, but I had to come back to look for you. I had been watching you for long but never could muster up the courage to talk to you. But then that day, you bumped into me and I was grateful to fate. I wanted to tell you but then that day you said you hated me. Please, please forgive me, I am not Maria, I'm Sera!" she sobbed. He reached out and held her in his arms, "I will Sera. If you marry me, then I will".

Together they walked out side by side out of the ward, a white cane and crutch in harmony. He smiled as she painted pictures of the old man wheezing in the bed, the woman in the red dress sitting on the bench, the high corridors, huge windows and the fat matron refusing to attend to the annoying patient standing at her desk. Past the green curtains flowing in the breeze flapping against the white walls covered with stains, down the green lawns with the broken benches, the gate with its drowsy tea-drinking watchman. Out onto the road they went laughing, towards a new life together.

●●●

## 20

# Edge of insanity

race could not believe that her mother had died and stared at Sona, the nurse, crying and then smirking, as she covered the body with a sheet. "She is only the nurse, damn it. I should be crying as it is my mother who just died. So then, why are my tears frozen", thought Grace. That day at the hospital the doctors had a meeting. They were sure that Dr. Shiv was overreacting. The deaths in the past few months on Sona's watch did not mean something was amiss. They asked him to leave it alone but Dr. Shiv's was determined to find out the truth. He continued to read the records of the night shift. Sona's shift.

The mystery was making him uneasy and he knew he had to put his suspicions to rest, so he went to the neighbours to find out more about her. They told him she had been deserted by her husband and children few years ago. Her neighbours called her aggressive and unhelpful. Just the other day, they said the old lady living on the first floor had slipped down the stairs. She refused to help when they asked her to, and had walked away saying she was better off dead. She worked at the near by hospital, or so she said and then suddenly one fine day her interest in the neighbours had begun to take on scary heights. She had become obsessed with diagnosing them as they sat talking in the garden in the evenings. Most would get up and move away the moment they saw her coming and the kids complained to their mothers that she would often grab and hug them calling them by her own children's names. No one wanted to have anything to do with her and when they all got together against her, she had stopped talking to them and they were glad.

At the hospital, Dr. Shiv stopped by the other nurses that day and asked them about her. They did not like her, they said. She made decisions for them and rude comments on their competence. She never came to the morning meetings and she even skipped briefings and seemed most unconcerned when her patients did not make it. She seemed to thrive on death and the wailing of relatives crying over their loved ones. The other nurses knew she manipulated shifts at the hospital and would often spend long hours on the ward during her night shift, insisting that her attention was important to the patients. In the past few weeks, three of her older patients did not make it through the night. Eighty-year-old Mrs. Chatterjee only had a broken hip, while Mr. Bose had been down with a mild fever and Rita was not that old to die of pneumonia.

And then that night came when the corridors were filled with children and women vomiting and lifeless. She flitted from one to another enjoying the tension filled air, as she shoved others aside peering into the victims eyelids. Dr. Shiv watched her ecstatic face at every wail piercing through the ward. Soon everything was lost in the urgency of the moment as the nurses and doctors ran around, loosing some and saving some. Death knocked on the doors as the wails grew stronger in the corridors. The food they all had eaten at a wedding was taking its toll. Fifteen children and five adults lay lifeless in the morgue, and many more lay on the beds sick, and soon the hospital corridors fell silent.

Dr. Shiv did not believe that any nurse could be as uncaring as Sona seemed to be. Something was not right with her. Late that night, he walked to the morgue and sat through the night reading the autopsy reports. The reports were unbelievable as the deadly medicine administered to each of the victims was the same. "How could that happen?" he thought, as he went down to the stores to check the medicines in the storeroom. Nothing seemed wrong, the injection bottles were full and the caps were intact. They were lined up the way they should have been, but then, why were they lying on two separate shelves? He picked up one from the top shelf and there seemed nothing amiss. He picked one from the second shelf up to the light, as if asking it to speak, when a very tiny drop fell onto his cheek. He peered closer at the tiny needle holes in the cap of the bottle. He pulled out the injections from the second shelf and placed them out on the table, slowly checking each one in the light. They all had been tampered with. The door banged open making him jump and drop the bottle on the floor. There she was standing against it, a knife in her hand. "You are such a pain. You should not have come down here. Oh, you are so dead" she said. "You will not get away from me". Dr. Shiv grabbed the chair holding it in front of him and screamed at her. "What have you done? Why, why did you inject poison into bottles? . "Doctor, doctor, you should have left it alone," she said. "You are going to kill me and then what, bury me in the store room? You are finished you mad woman." said Dr. Shiv.

"Dr. Shiv, Dr. Shiv, it's the store room, you know, and I'm in charge. It's my world, my home and you dare to ask me, how and why?" she screamed, "In what world are you living. Do you not see the suffering of the human race? Oh, but you are a doctor and you save lives. That's fine by me. Have I ever stopped you, but save lives of whom and why? Do you ever stop to think whether you should save that life lying in front of you or not. No, you don't, but I do? Every day someone or the other is leaving behind their family members behind to suffer. Like I am suffering! Tell me why did he leave me? I spent my whole life looking after him. Even my children did nothing to stop him but walked out with him. That Mrs. Chatterjee only broke a hip and the family left her here to lie in the bed for months. Did they take her home when she was better? No, her daughter-in-law says, "let's leave her here for some more time and we can take her home when we are back from our holiday". She had to break her hip, she had said, just as they were to leave. May I ask, who were they going to leave her with when they planned that holiday in the first place? Huh!!! And Mr. Bose, what was his fault? He only had a jaundice fever but did his son take him home. No! How was he going to manage the special care he needed. The hospital was there was it not for that? That lady Rita, that old man in the general ward, that patient in ward six, the husband lying in a coma not knowing his wife died in the accident, that old lady sitting by her sick husband. Why, why, all the suffering," Sona babbled incoherently.

Dr. Shiv stared in horror at her and as she turned to close the door, he quickly pressed numbers on the intercom and pressing the speaker on, raised his voice speaking as loudly as he could to cover the sound of the voice at the other end to pacify her. "Please don't be foolish. I understand you Sona, but why kill me. I won't say anything so let's just go out of the store room and let us talk this over," he said. "As if I am going to believe a snooping scoundrel like you", she said swiping his outstretched arm with a clean cut streaked across his forearm. Dr. Shiv screamed in pain grabbing his arm to stop the blood.

"I don't want to hurt you, but if I don't, then you will stop me from delivering people and all those poor neglected souls who will never go home. It was working fine, but no, you had to go snooping around", she screeched flinging the chair at him. Dr. Shiv fell back onto the floor just as the door behind her burst open, knocking her to the floor. Sona grappled the hands that held her screaming, "Let me go, Let me go. I had to deliver them from a life worse than death. I ended the suffering of those who no one wanted back home. I delivered them from neglect. I delivered them from loneliness and pain".

# 21

# Tired of hurting

The waves swirled around her feet, as she dug them deeper into the cold sand. Back and forth the waves curled around her feet, as they crashed towards the shore sliding back into the deep, to gather strength and crash to the shore. The waves angrily pushed against her, the sand tickling between her toes as if trying to shove her out of their way. Rani stood waiting for the waves to lash the shore and drag her with them to the grey foam rippling and swelling before her. Her thoughts raged endlessly like the noisy bleak and grey waves and as she looked at the two figures walking in the distance a calm came over her. She sat down at the edge of the sand watching the sun go down.

Her thoughts flew back to the day she first met Roop. Handsome, tall with the deepest brown eyes she had ever seen and a smile that lighted up the entire classroom. She stood there, books in her arms, waiting to enter a class full of people she did not know and there he was smiling and beckoning her to sit next to him. She never knew when the lecture ended, his elbow touching her, or was it that she had moved closer. He introduced her to his friends and then one day he dropped on his knees and asked her to be his girlfriend. They were in love, each more possessive of the other. Or was it that he was the one more possessive than her. As the days passed things began to slowly change. Her friends warned her but she had no time for them. She loved eating on the roadside but soon it was a thing of the past as was walking to college with her friends, talking to them on phone, watching movies or participating in college shows. She did not mind changing, after all women change for the man they love and those were such insignificant things. She did not take him home to her parents, but the day she did; they did not approve. "Roop is not the man for you, you have changed. You are no more the girl we brought up", they reasoned. She rubbished their worries and went on to become whatever he wanted. Sit and she would sit. Stand, so be it, and she would stand up for him. Her world was his love and his word the gospel truth. They had their share of fights and of course she was always the one who was always wrong and apologized each time. Then one day, Roop took her home to meet his family. They turned up their nose at her. She cried into her pillow that night as her parents stood in the door watching her and pleading with her not to make a mistake.

Roop's parents threatened to disown him if he married her, but he was adamant. The room in the chawl they bought was small and cute and she was so happy in her tiny world. Her parents visited when Roop was not home and as she laid her tired head on her mother's shoulder, her mother begged her, "Rani, please study further. You must be able to stand on your own. What in case something goes wrong." "Nothing is going to go wrong, Mother. I am happy and he takes good care of me", Rani argued but soon buckled under their pressure with a promise that Roop should never get to know that she was studying. He had warned her that he would leave her if she ever worked. It was so wrong, she knew that, but she loved him and did not want to loose him. The days just seemed to fly as she continued to study loving every minute of it. She wanted to share her success with Roop, but she dreaded his wrath hiding that degree in the deep crevices of her cupboard. Months passed as she pleaded with him to allow her to work, but like a man possessed, he consumed her time, her life, her every being. As life moved on and the pressures of life began to show cracks, he blamed her for every failure of his, and every disappointment and as time passed the beatings grew worse. She had given him two sons who never seemed to care about her endless selfless love for them. Her life went on and on, serving the men in her life. The strands on her forehead turned silver but he would not allow her the luxury of a few stolen moments for herself. She watched women her age strutting around like peacocks, in their finery, as she shook the endless clothes onto the clothesline. She had no time for neighbours and they never knocked on her door except for Shanta. Shanta, her dear confidante and her understanding husband Ram. Shanta, who had helped her fill out the exam forms, help her study and shared her problems over endless cups of tea.

Roop never spoke to the neighbours and even her sons seemed to make fewer friends and more enemies by the day. He never knew about her friendship with Shanta and she would not tell him. She knew he would stop her from meeting her. Breakfast to dinner and dinner to breakfast, her life ran like the hands of the clock. Then one night, exhausted and feverish, she made the cardinal sin of saying no to his overtures. That night the beating never stopped till she shriveled up and cried in pain as he dragged her out of the house and slammed the door on her. She lay there in the dark covering in the shadows hoping no one would see and unable to move.

Things were never the same from that day onwards as the beatings continued at the slightest provocation, and soon her sons were turning against her too. He found fault in the food she made, the clothes she ironed, the beds she made. He fought for everything and hit her for everything and then one day, in an unexplainable wrath she beat him back as hard as she could unmindful of his strength. His fury knew no bounds as he kicked her over and over again and again till she collapsed in the corner of the room. She lay there crying broken knowing she could not go back to her parents even if she wanted to. They had died broken hearted a long time ago.

Rani knew now for sure that she dare not let him know about the few hours at work that she looked forward to each day. Each morning she waited for him and the boys to leave and slipped out each time taking a different doorway, a different street, a different bus stop, mortified that he might be waiting and watching. She would be back before they returned ready to serve them. 26th July was just an ordinary rainy day, but as afternoon came, the streets turned into rivers and Rani stood at the office window wondering how she was going to get home before them. Drenched and fearful, she stood at the door as his eyes bored into her very being. "You wretched woman, how dare you leave the home. I'm going to kill you today, I'm going to kill you today" screamed Roop and the beating continued late into the night. "Hit me as much as you like..kill me for all I care but I am not going to give up my job", she cried in pain. Soon Roop did not seem to care anymore. Now all he wanted was the money she brought in. She lied about her salary, hiding part of it and keeping it away safe with Shanta.

Rani looked up from her desk, turning numb as she watched him having animated conversations with her office colleagues sipping coffee. She was lucky to have such a good husband they said, as they thumped him on the back and waved them off. As soon as the latch in the door turned, he turned upon her as his eyes narrowed pouncing on her. He grabbed her by the hair hitting and flinging her about like a rag doll. Rani cried in pain shouting to her sons for help her, eyes turning to stone as they held her down to be kicked again and again by Roop. Her soul cracked, the storm in her chest burst into a raging cloud of hatred. Pushing them away with all her might, she grabbed the stick lying in the corner and lashed out at them, cursing them over and over again. The tears streamed down, as she rained blows on them over and over again. The neighbours came running and soon everything was calm.

Shanta held her close and they walked to the police station. Rani dropped her weary head onto the table as Shanta wrote out the complaint. They pleaded with her to drop the charges. As she walked away, she promised them a punishment that would be a lesson to all those women who think that their husbands and sons are Gods. 'Why did the roads of women's lives only stretch from the door of the house to the kitchen and to the bedroom? Why can't our likes, dislikes, wants and needs be important and why can't the men respect us as individuals?', she thought. That night the house was empty and calm as her heart had never been before. She felt alive for the first time.

The dark golden sea caressed her feet, as she sat there watching her saviors, her friends, Shanta and Ram walking up to her. A smile flitted across her face as Shanta sat down next to her on the cool sand and laid a comforting arm around her shoulder. Her tears had dried and her heart was as calm like the setting sun before her. The sun had set on her sorrows and a new moon had risen. It was time to live, time to live for her, her own self!

●●●

95

## 22

# Flames of shame

There was no fire in her room, only smoke was billowing through the crack of her door. Manjula slowly moved to the door, carefully opening and gasped as the smoke filled her lungs. It seemed to clear as she peered down the hallway seeing nothing but darkness. She breathed into the wet towel she held as the smoke clouded her vision. The fire fighters came through the smoke and carried her out from windows and over broken parapets, as the thick smoke billowed around them like grey clouds on a dark rainy day. Soon the building was completely engulfed in flames. She struggled painfully through the night holding out her hand to Dr. Maneckan as if wanting to say something but he silenced her, frantically to save her. She made it through the night but lay there weak and convulsing begging for a piece of paper and pen. Dr. Maneckan stared at the words "Help me, my brothers want me dead. I am not depressed or mad. They set my home on fire". He knew now that it was their doing and they had wanted her dead. She was the only one who could destroy them. The family inheritance had been passed on to her and she did not even care. Manjula wanted to sell everything. They had worked too hard to let her just walk in and take over their lives. Her brothers had said that she had been depressed and set fire to the house.

He held out the note she had written calling them her murderers. Soon tempers flared and they pressed their heel into the lifeline holding her together, watching her thin body convulsing into silence. Dr. Maneckan eyes widened in horror as he desperately tried to free himself from the hands that clamped his mouth and held him down. The letter disappeared into smoke as the hospital corridors buzzed in unison blaming him for her death. A clear case of malpractice they said. She had recovered well, so then how did she suddenly convulse and die.

He saw images shimmered and warped in the ever-growing haziness as he paced the night streets not knowing where he was going. He stood hiding from the pouring rain watching the fuzzy headlights of the cars as they zipped past with the colours of the neon shop lights flickering bright colours on his face. Wet and huddled, people stared back from across the street as he turned to the couple standing next to him, sharing half a smile. He was worried now. If only he had not gloated and shown them the letter. The reflections in the puddles near his feet changed shapes and slowly he started to enjoy the shapes it took as running people and cars rippled the water. The changing shapes in the water suddenly seemed like a sign from heaven. May be he just needed to look at the facts in a new way and maybe there was a way out. He stood there thinking for long but he knew that there was no way out of this shame but death. He sighed as he pulled up the collar of his coat and stepped out into the dark wet streets. He was not going down without taking them down too. He walked into the manor and as they sat there laughing at him, he shot them one by one.

97

Dr. Maneckan turned the gun and shot himself in the stomach, but the wound was not deep enough. He struggled like a fish out of water flopping around on the floor and trying to get to his feet as his body began to feel it was floating. The headache was back and this time he could hear rattling sounds louder than a train screeching over the tracks. He couldn't reach for the gun lying on the ground as he groaned in pain. He waited for death to come. It had to come before they came to get him. The room began to spin like a top, and black wormlike spots danced in front of his eyes as he tried to shake them from his head. The pain began to dim as he lay there waiting for it to end, but then why was he still alive?

He lay there staring at the cell door that had just been slammed in his face. "I had nothing to do with it. It was her brothers, they killed her. They deserved to die. I was innocent", he screamed but no one believed him. He was sentenced for malpractice and murder. Even death had cheated him, and there had been no way out.

●●●

# 23

# The crushed rose

Maria watched the sky change colours as the sun waved its goodbye and sank slowly into the water as dusk crawled its way across the waves onto the sand. Involuntarily touching the scars on her face, she stared at her shadow on the sand slowly disappearing, hoping that she could too. The sands of darkness stretched around her as the sea darkened. She slowly walked into the sea, her lifeless body soon floating in the dark as she gasped her last goodbyes. Dawn came and there Maria lay on the warm sand, her hands outstretched to the sky and her face serene and calm.

Who is she? Wondered the police as they walked past the lifeless woman lying there in the far end of the corner covered in white. It was going to be a long time before they could unravel this one, there had been nothing on her to tell her story but the scars and a bracelet with an inscription of a rose, and a birthday greeting engraved on it clasped tightly in her hand.

At first it was unnerving. The middle aged man sitting alone at a nearby table had been staring at her since he walked in. If she looked at him, he immediately buried his face in the menu. Rose tried to ignore him, but she was sure he was trying to check her out. She grimaced thinking 'what a pervert', considering he was old enough to be her father. She had never ever been stared at in such a compelling manner since a long time. It reminded her of the woman hiding in the bushes outside her home watching her. No one had seemed to notice her, but Rose knew she was there and many a times she waved her hand wickedly at her. Then one day the woman had just disappeared never to return.

Rose turned and unnerved the man staring back at him. He jumped up nervously and his elbow hit the table hard and as he gasped the table overturned. The waiters came running as he turned away embarrassed and red-faced.

Rose loved her evening jog and even more being the only person in the world on that stretch. Not this evening, however, she thought. Through the dense green trees far beyond, she could glimpse a figure now and again running alongside her. She shrugged and jogged past the old man sitting on the bench holding tight, the hand of a thin frail women sitting with her head slumped into her chest. "I have seen her somewhere" thought Rose as the old man caught her eye. Then as if he had lost courage buried his head into his coat as the frail woman looked at her with unseeing eyes. A shiver ran down her spine when suddenly the elusive figure appeared ahead of her. It was the man from the diner, she was sure of it. She had to be sure, so she picked up her pace as she ran past, pretending not to notice him. Out of the corner of her eye, she could see he was definitely there for her.

She ran into the line of trees and picked up a large stick pretended to pause for breath, waiting for him to catch up, ready to strike him if he attacked her, but he seemed to have disappeared. Well, catch you at the diner, she thought as she let out a sigh of relief. She continued to run, holding onto the large stick and as she retraced her steps, she saw the old man clasping his chest, the blood flowing down his left sleeve down over the back of his wrist. "Where was the woman?" she thought, as she turned to see her vanishing in the distance down the path towards the sea. Helpless, Rose turned to help the old man to his feet as she watched the man from the diner run away.

Rose watched the doctors through the small glass opening of the operating room glass. She could not see what they were doing but she knew they had managed to remove the bullet. He could not be her grandfather or could he be? she wondered, as he took her hand. Pointing to the silver bracelet with the engraved rose dangling on her wrist, he asked her to read out the words inside it. It would read 'to my daughter on her eighteenth birthday', he said, and indeed it did. "How did you know? I was given this by my parents on my eighteenth birthday," Rose said. "That was made by your mother for you. Maria sent you one and kept a similar one with her to remind her of you. She never removed the bracelet ever", replied her grandmother. "But I have parents and I have never met her or seen her before", said Rose. "You did! She watched over you every single day of her life" she said holding out a photograph for her to see. Rose's eyes widened as the face she used to see each day behind the bushes smiled back at her. "That's the woman I saw running into the sea too." Grandmother began to sob as she held out another photo for Rose to see. Rose stared in horror at the man in the photo her grandmother held asking if she had seen him ever. "This is the man I saw at the diner this morning", she screamed, "I am sure he must have shot grandfather. I guess he saw me coming and ran away".

"This man in the photo is the son of your grandfather's partner. We tried to keep Maria away from him, but it was too late and when she told us she was having his baby, we could do nothing. They were married in a hurry and one day he disappeared leaving a note blaming her for his misfortunes and disinheritance." said grandmother. "Then why did you give me up?" asked Rose. "We were scared of telling you the truth. Actually, he was not your father. Your mother had a miscarriage when he left her and we got her married to a fine man, your father; but God had other plans and your father died leaving your mother distraught. She went into depression and began to harm you and tried to kill you many a times. We had to get you away from her and sent you to live with a couple we trusted."

"That man found out about you and threatened to harm you and your mother. Your mother was already sinking further into a depression and one day in a fit of rage he scarred your mother and ran away swearing revenge on us. We knew we had to tell you everything soon, so that you could protect yourself from him. Your mother was getting out of control and in her depressive state, kept asking to see you. Your grandfather knew you jogged in the park, so he decided to bring her there just to see you once, hoping that it might help her state of mind. They did not know that he was already there stalking you, but I guess he saw them sitting there and shot your grandfather instead. Come now, we must go and bring your mother home." Grandmother said as she broke down crying. Rose stared at the lifeless woman lying there in the far end of the corner covered in white. She lifted the sheet and cried for the scars, and the bracelet with an inscription of a rose and birthday greeting engraved on it, clasped tightly around her hand.

●●●

## 24

# A prank too far

Kamal was one of a kind who never conformed to society. She loved her freedom and her life rotated around her mother and friends. She was a tomboy in every sense of the word, with a no-nonsense and stubborn streak that even her friends could not get past. Being with her was like being on a roller coaster ride with no light at the end of the tunnel. She was a whirlwind of energy, tall and athletic, while Mira and their other friend Shana were her loyal and loving side-kicks. Neither dared to question her, though they never needed to, as their friendship was like three swans, flying one behind the other on a clear sky in complete unison, to new horizons. Everyday, lunchtime at work was a new adventure with a new thrill for the three friends. Whether it was walking together to the sea side close to their office, or chattering over sweet corn on a rainy day or sharing lunch at a cafe. Of course, it was Kamal who decided where they were going and Mira would never ask where because she would just be told to follow. Follow she did with a laugh and a bit of grumbling, for it did not matter as they always ended up having fun. Picnics meant up the mountains or off the beaten track but never on the beach, for Kamal hated getting wet in the salty sea and even more, standing around in the sun on the hot sand. Mira loved her friendship with Kamal and the table tennis games, picnics and fun together with her, were her break away from the daily stress of work and home. Kamal, Shana and Mira, like the Three Stooges or Three Amigos, enjoyed their companionship and friendship to the fullest. They had other friends in the group but somehow the three of them were always together. Shana was a short cute dumpling of a girl with an infectious laughter while Mira was a 'fun loving, friendly, ready to try anything new' type of girl. Kamal on the other hand, was every bit stubborn and held her ground in most things and always got her way. She did not believe in being there for parties or dressing up for events, happy just whistling to her favourite songs. Different in so many things and so many ways, yet something unexplainable tied them together.

Then one day it changed. Kamal began to freeze her friends out and disappear in the lunchtime alone to visit family or that's what she used to tell Mira. Mira, a firm believer in friendship never forced her hand, or questioned her till it became too frequent. Besides Kamal had always been a prankster and it had been many times that she had taken Mira for a ride up the prank path. Like sitting outside the window at the holiday home covered in toothpaste scaring friends, or hiding under the bed in the middle of the night and knocking on it to scare them. Shana had always been the one to break into laughter, so Mira knew how to get out the truth. Mira never believed half the things Kamal would say but that day Mira broke down when Shana told her that Kamal had a tumor in the brain and swore her to secrecy. This time Shana was not laughing. Mira's world crashed as she struggled to find ways to find out more but Kamal being who she was, shrugged her off with her usual no-nonsense behavior.

Kamal's afternoon visits to the doctor increased and she refused to allow her friends to be with her. March 21st was the day of the operation, she said, and Mira begged to be with her, but Kamal refused to share details and even Shana could do nothing. Mira began to feel helpless and morose, as the days passed while on the other hand Shana seemed to take it well. They could do nothing because Kamal did not want them with her.

As the day drew close, Mira began to lose her appetite, losing sleep, worrying, even her husband could not console her. She kept on begging Shana to tell her more but Shana had nothing to tell and Kamal had crawled into a shell with occasional phone calls. That dreaded day dawned and it was also Mira's new year day but she was not in the mood to celebrate as she waited for news from the hospital. Scared out of her wits when the phone rang, she begged her husband to answer it. Her husband picked up the phone to find Kamal at the end of the line wishing him a happy new year. Mira was shell-shocked. Her heart stopped as her husband admonished Kamal for making his wife cry. This time Shana had managed to keep the prank going without laughing but Mira had died a thousand deaths since that day. If Mira could have crawled down that telephone wire she would have gladly done so, to tie it around Kamal's neck and strangle her. "A prank?" she screamed, "a prank?". This time it had gone too far and that day Kamal lost a friend forever.

●●●

## 25

# Twins in the ashes

Abandoned outside on the steps of the police station late at night, while the constable slept blissfully unaware, the twins lay there boxing their fists into the night sky. Dawn broke with the sound of the motorcycle roaring into the compound to the accompaniment of their loud wails. The old constable broke out of his slumber, straightened his clothes rubbing his eyes vigorously as his superior placed the little girls on the table.

They stood around staring at the two little girls, wondering what to do. "Let's call this one Chirutha," said the old constable twirling his moustache "and this one Mathura". The constables looked up in disdain at the constable who hurriedly explained, "My grandmother's names". Now that the naming ceremony seemed done, the other constables moved away leaving the old constable to take charge.

Chirutha stared at her disfigured face in the mirror, threw her bag on the floor and burst into tears. It was never going to be an ordinary day ever for her, she knew. She stared into the darkness of cold and frigid night. Who said living in a foster home was easy? She could not believe that purposefully creating a nuisance, and hurting herself time and again, was helping

Mathura. Getting beaten by the foster mother till she fell on the floor into a semi unconscious state had become a frequent thing and Mathura seemed to care no more. Chirutha knew she had to do something. She just could not watch her twin hurting herself anymore, for every lash crushed her soul. After all, they were twins. Mathura had felt the same for her, the day the acid was thrown on Chirutha's face by their foster sister. It had hardened each crevice of Chirutha's heart as "escape, escape" were the only words that kept ticking in her mind. Both sisters knew that they had to leave soon, but how? It was not for lack of trying for sure, as they sat there, recalling the first time they had tried. Then there was danger and hunger lurking around the corner. The foster mother was after all getting a good sum of money for their care and then one day the money stopped. Threatening to hurt them if they did not leave she threw them out. They had nothing and nowhere to go. Not even the orphanage. It had burnt down long ago.

The box flew open as her foster mother flung it across the room and that night the sisters rummaged through the box looking for clues to their past. A half torn letter floated to the floor, as Chirutha stared at the words swimming before her. Her hands clutched the letter as she ran across the street, her heart beat harder than before as she dialed the number.

The two sisters walked out of the house into the freezing cold night, as their foster mother watched from behind the curtains happy to see them go. The old constable was waiting and smiled at the two homeless girls on his doorstep and invited them into his home. The skies seemed bluer as Chirutha watched Mathura bloom under the loving care of the old constable and his handsome son. Chirutha sat at the window with a smile on her face, watching them share tender looks. She was not jealous. No, she was not. She was sure of that. Mathura had started to work while Chirutha got turned down everywhere she went. No one was comfortable with a scarred face around them, and as days passed, it seemed like things had reversed with the twins. Mathura had become her and she had become Mathura. Chirutha could not believe that hurting herself time and again was helping her just like it had her sister, at the foster home. The old constable tried his best to help her, but Chirutha withdrew into a shell. Sitting on the window sill, watching the world go by was her life. Days turned into months with Chirutha waiting for Mathura to return from work each day and tell her all about it, but soon Mathura had no time for her. Mathura had begun to avoid her and leave her out of her life. The loneliness was beginning to eat her, and her mind was played games with her.

Her head began to spin, as she stared at the dark red sticky substance on her hand. It could not be blood she thought? She turned in horror and stared at Mathura flopping on the floor like a fish out of water and die. The cold eyes of Mathura lying on crumpled on the floor stared back at her unblinking, as Chirutha screamed and screamed. Funnily enough she couldn't remember what happened. All they had been doing was talking, until the talking turned ugly. That exact sentence that turned into a storm seemed so insignificant now, then why she had stuck the paper knife into Mathura's neck, she couldn't fathom. All she could remember was her twin's smug face teasing her relentlessly about her crumpled ugly face. No one and nothing could break her, she had thought, but jealousy had done her in. Twins were supposed to understand and feel each other's pain, then why had Mathura not cared. She stood there in the dark dingy cell, staring at the barred window, as memories of games they played, the food they stole from the kitchen at the foster home in the dark of the night, cuddling up to each other for comfort came rushing back. Chirutha knew her life had no meaning now. She had killed her own sister, her twin.

●●●

**26**

# No remorse

She sat on the rocking chair in the verandah, staring into the nothingness of her garden overlooking the sea. The bright magenta morning glory flowers curled into a deep sleep, hugging the vines. The bright red shoe flower raised its head to sky and dropped into slumber, as the sun sank into the ocean and disappeared. The creaking of the rocking chair resounded the stillness of the night and then, there was complete silence. "What a life, I am so blessed, to live life as I wish and to have so many friends who love me for who I am", she said to herself. Friends often confessed that she was a whirlwind of fun that brought a breath of laughter and madness to their lives. She loved living life to its fullest, unlike many of her friends who had stopped much before their hair could turn silver. So what if her son did not care to be there for her?

Her friends had cautioned her that the saying that 'a son is a son till he gets a wife' always is true, but she had scoffed, saying she only believed in giving and would never be asking for anything all her life. She remembered how her cute five year old Vivaan only got out of bed for school if she yelled 'boat in the sea'. He loved boats and even as a kid would sit on the verandah, looking out into sea. A captain on the ship is what he wanted to be. It had not been easy for her to convince her husband, as they were working to pay off debts they had taken to make a home, but she was determined to fulfill her son's dream. Besides what was her purpose in life, if not to give her son his dream and make him happy? Her world almost fell apart the day her husband died unexpectedly but she stood strong and picked herself up. Days morphed into years and patience won, as she waited for her son to stand shoulder to shoulder, and help her through life's burdens, but it was not to be. She still remembered the day he came home and gave her a tight hug just two months of getting a job and said "she said yes, mom!" That became the darkest day in her life as she lost her son forever. She still could not find it in herself to blame her son, after all, men will be men. It's the woman who has to strengthen the bonds, like she did for her husband. She recalled how she loved her amazingly strong and loving father-in-law, who had always been there for her and when he moved away, she had pushed her husband to take care of him and be there for him at any cost. Maybe she did not teach her son those values, or maybe he just did not learn them well enough. Who knew better than her, that she had done her duty to her son and that's all that ever mattered to her. Besides she always had lived life her way. So now it was his turn to live life on his terms. He moved away. She did not need his money, but somewhere in the corner of her heart she hoped he would care enough to ask, pick up a phone or to drop by often and give her a hug. To hear his voice and a warm tight hug was all she craved for but he never seemed to have the time for her. Life was not meant for wondering why, she knew; but some days she questioned herself whether her philosophy of "live and let live" and "forgive and forget" were worth living by. Maybe she should have made demands on his time and money. Maybe she should have taken that first pay cheque from him, instead of saying "you earned it". May be she should have demanded he repay the loan she took for his dream, instead of saying it was her duty. Mothers, she thought, always worrying about their children and not themselves. Just maybe she should have hated him for what he did to her. If only she could, she sighed as she stood up staring at the dark waves lashing to the shore.

She walked into the house and as she touched her husband's garlanded photo, his words came rushing back, "See, I told you so". Picking up his photo and admonishing him with a smile, she said, "You know me well. I am not one to waste time lamenting what could have been, or worrying about what will be. I will always find good in each and every thing. You know that I have and always will live life king size. So hubby dear, I shall sing as I drive to work with the windows rolled down without a care in the world. I will make new friends every day and make others happy. I shall eat dessert every single day or jump off a plane without a parachute, or dance on a crowded street, if I feel like it." The silvery moon rose high in the sky, smiling down upon 'the mother', the most unique and precious gift of God to mankind.

●●●

27

# There is a ghost in the house

"This is my house," she cried out, "not something I am going to give up". Sherry sighed as she stared into the darkness. Karly slept peacefully by her side. Her two brothers had been at logger-heads fighting to sell the house. It had lied unkempt and wasted, like their mother who lived there alone after Malcom, her youngest brother had died. Besides, everything Sherry owned had been sold after the untimely death of her husband at war, so where could she go now? Mother needed her and she needed a home for Karly. Karly, the little orphan of her dead friend she had brought home and into her heart. Poor Karly, she thought, it was becoming difficult for her to believe in his ghost stories, but then the state of the house did not help his imagination either.

Karly stood at the gate of the school and hesitantly walked into the classroom full of curious faces staring at him. No one wanted anything to do with him. Besides, he saw ghosts or so he said, but no one believed him, not even mother. Only Grammy did, as he cuddled up to her each night, and talked to her about the ghost he saw. She believed him, she said. The boys had ganged up on him and refused to allow him to play, as he sat on the school bench, watching them play. The ball flew out over his head, and he turned to see it disappear into bushes and fall into the creek beyond the school boundary. The boys came running over scrambling in the bushes looking for the ball, but he was not going to tell. Then it happened. Mickey turned to Karly and asked him if he had seen where it had landed. He jumped up to help them search, knowing that they would never find it. That day at school he had a spring in his step but not for long. "There is a ghost in my house", he whispered to Mickey, "and he talks to me". Mickey burst out laughing. "I am not lying. I see him every night, you jerk", said Karly his face turning blue with rage. "Prove it!" the other kids cried, and beat him up screaming "liar liar". That day the teacher called Sherry and told her that her son was losing his mind.

With a determined look, she got up and stormed out, "How dare she say such things? How could she be so cold? So mean to suggest that Karl was losing his mind." She was restless that day as she walked around the old house for a while, straightening the cushions, touching the family photos lined up on the mantelpiece, feeling the warm dust on her fingertips soothing her troubled mind. She played with the dust on her fingertips till all was calm.

Karly lay awake in his bed, unable to shake the laughing boys faces out of his mind. He raised his hands, making dark shadows on the wall in the light of the moon falling on it and screamed as a shadow fell on it and disappeared. Sherry woke up with a start to find Karly lying drenched in sweat and as she clasped him in her arms, he fell unconscious. It was days before he woke and when he did, all he did was whisper "the ghost in the house is coming to get me. He talks to me about you, mother. Even grammy talks to him". Sherry turned to look at her stone-faced mother who admonished the little boy for lying and imagining things.

Sherry lay down in her bed stroking Karly's tousled head and soon the house was soon covered in darkness. It had stopped raining but the clouds were banging against each other in the sky making loud scary unnerving noises. Was it the flash of lightening or was it the clashing of thunder? Sherry didn't know what woke her up as she froze in horror staring at the figure standing by her mother's bedside. A tall man in a huge overcoat stood there, his face covered with a muffler. She sprang out of bed and lunged at him ripping off the muffler staring into deep dark blue eyes as her mother screamed in horror.

Malcolm stood there staring at her, and with a swift move, pushed her away and jumped out into the darkness. Sherry ran to the balcony staring out into the darkness but she could see nothing. Malcolm? It couldn't be her brother, Malcolm, she thought as she sat down on the chair. He was dead long time ago. Something was very wrong. Her mother turned away and wept.

Malcolm, her sweet gentle brother, whom she had loved so dearly and missed all these years. It had been a case of unrequited love gone too far. Sherry had tried to stop him from stalking her friend, Sheila, but he did not listen or maybe he just was not willing to let go. Sheila too, had implored him to leave her alone. After all, she was now married with a husband and child. He had just come back from the war, and maybe things had just reached a breaking point for him. They said he had stormed into her house and blown up her home in a deadly explosion killing all of them. Karly, their son, had survived because he had been at the neighbours playing. "He is not a ghost but he has feigned his death, and now he is back to kill Karly" she told the police but they laughed at her and told her to get proof. Mother begged her not to tell on him, but she could not let anything happen to Karly. She knew he would come back for Karly. That night she sat in the corner of the room in the darkness, waiting.

Karly cowered in Sherry's arms, staring at the face of the man that had haunted him,. Slowly, his fears left him and he looked up and smiled. 'Time to go home, Karly,' said Sherry as she turned for one last look at her brother. "Sherry, you have got to understand. I loved her and if I could not have her, no one could. She should have waited for me. Besides you know, it's very easy to fake your own death and get away with it, if you want. All I needed to do was to keep changing my disguise and keep moving away". Malcom said. "Sheila never loved you, and you knew that Malcom. She did not need to die". Sherry retorted as he continued, "but there was no point in repenting after the deed was done, was there? Besides, coming back home from the dead, that's not so easy. I walked past you in the street so many times mustering courage to speak to you, Sherry. To tell you that I am there for you and won't let our brothers harm you. I spoke to you at the market, but you never recognized me in my disguise. All I wanted was to be with mother and you for some time and disappear again. I never intended to harm Karly."

●●●

28

# She knew but....

Her journey to hell and back had begun a few months ago. Rita met him at her friend's house and fell hook, line and sinker in love despite the warning looks and hints. After all, love stories don't only happen at the movies. He was the most romantic and loving guy ever, or so she thought, till that devastating night. That night they had friends for a night over and she was so tired that she excused herself and went off to the bedroom to catch a bit sleep. Soon there was no sound of music and neither was he sleeping next to her. Worried, she walked out to see drunken bodies lying on the sofas and floor and there he was with another girl under the covers. Angry, betrayed and hurt, all she did was scream into the dark night as he stood there almost unashamed holding on tight to the girl's hand as everyone picked themselves up and left.

He began stalking her, sending messages telling her he was sorry and as the days turned to months, the messaged turned to threats. She told him it was over but he would not let her be. It felt like she was on this roller coaster that she couldn't get off. Rita tried to ignore him, but every corner she turned, there he was. She had moved home but he had found her and soon she dared not step out of the house. The curtains of her room remained drawn, as she occasionally peeped into the street to find him standing there at the corner, staring up at her window. The doorbell had not stopped ringing throughout the day and every time she peered into the peep hole his grim face stared back at her. He screamed each time he banged on the door, "It's not over". She turned white as she took a step backwards sitting down on the chair, a slight panic started to set in. Three days had passed now and she had been holed up in the house.

She did not know what to do. After all she knew and had done nothing then. Her head pained, as she recalled that deadly night she had found him with another woman. He had tried to explain that nothing was meant to happen between him and his estranged wife but things had just got out of hand. Rita refused to listen and locked herself in the bedroom. She stood staring out into the dark night as the voices from the other room turned louder. His wife was threatening to kill herself and soon neighbours barged in to intervene. Soon all was quiet and as she sat there sobbing in the arms of her husband, the neighbours left with satisfied smiles on their faces. They sat there talking for hours. Rita watched them, wondering what would become of her in this mess. The dark of the night seemed to grow darker and then it happened. Rita's eyes widened in horror as he turned on his wife tightening his stranglehold on her and stuffed a napkin into her mouth to muffle her screams. Rita stood rooted to the floor as she watched her flopping around like a rag doll in his hand. He dragged his wife to the open window and as she struggled to escape his deadly grip; he pulled out the stuffed cloth from her mouth and threw her over. Her scream rented the night air, as she plummeted twelve stories down to her death. Rita turned to stone staring at him, hiding in folds of the curtains watching the crowd collect near her crumpled body lying in the compound.

She had wanted to believe that he was free because he was proven innocent. Those unsuspecting neighbours vouched for her suicidal behaviour that night. She knew it was a web of lies. Accomplices, and they were in it together. She had begun to believe that she was responsible and that everything was her fault. If only she had asked them to leave. If only she had not seen him kill her. If only she had told the truth, she thought to herself. The walls seemed closing in on her tight, and she knew she had to end it. Rita picked up the phone and dialed the police.

●●●

**29**

# Broken wings

Devi stared at the message on her mobile, and with a sigh just blocked her son forever. The little one-bedroom flat was nothing compared to the huge five-bedroom house she had left behind, but she was happy. A whole new world had opened up for her. She had a spring in her step as she walked down to the community hall. Her thoughts flew back in time.

She knew there was no point in arguing any further. Latika was not going to understand, as all that mattered to her, was her opinions and beliefs. "I have been brought up to forgive family. I firmly believe in the importance of living and let live", Devi told her friend. "But this is going too far," her friend, Asha, reasoned with her, "It is your house and you are not allowed to do anything your way. You are not dependent on them and yet they stop you from going out with your friends. Why?" Devi grimaced and turned away. They had been married for over eight months now and yet Latika never seemed to grow up. Manipulating her husband with emotional blackmail was her weapon, though 'she never said anything, you see!' All she did was tell him 'don't ask me, do what you wish'. Which man, reasoned Devi, wished to come home to a grumpy wife? It became easier by the day for him to avoid confrontations by simply ignoring his mother at home.

It is an unspoken rule in any household that the day the daughter-in-law walks into the house, it becomes her home. Latika wanted to have her cake and eat it too. She found ways to keep her husband away from his mother, and filled his head with stories of the evil mother-in-law who troubled her when he was away. Devi surprisingly, never found it in her heart to say anything and kept on forgiving her son for ignoring her. The emotional blackmail had worked its magic. Latika had built around her, walls of selfishness, and wanted things done her way. It was always about her. Devi knew her son's biggest fault was not showing his emotions, but she knew that under that 'I don't care attitude', Raj did care, but was helpless as all men are when it comes to wives.

Perhaps women were meant to retire and bring up their grandchildren, but Devi had been waiting to live her life the way she wanted, after her retirement. Proud of her son, she had welcomed Latika, but she knew now that Latika only chose to seek her out, when she needed something. A spoilt girl who did not want her mother-in-law around, but running the household expenses was Devi's responsibility. Latika never allowed Raj to give his mother money saying it was her right to enjoy, and if things did not go her way she made sure Devi was insulted and ignored. As the days passed, Devi found herself confined to one of the five bedrooms in the house. Life became more and more difficult for her, as she had nothing left to do. One fine morning things came to a head, and Devi asked them to move out of the house. Latika refused and demanded she move out, threatening to get her arrested under the dowry act if she did not. Her son stood there unconcerned and Devi wondered what next. Devi knew what she had to do even if it meant giving in to their demands. After all she wanted to live her life and she knew it was not going to be easy to go on living a neglected life.

"We talk about women empowerment and being feminists, but the biggest mistake we make is teaching our sons that the wife should come first. 'Keeping her happy is all you need to do', is what we tell them. On the other hand we teach our daughters to serve the husband and look after the in-laws, as she would her own parents. Sadly Latika seemed to have got the first part but lost completely on the second part. They say 'a son is a son till he finds him a wife, a daughter's a daughter for the rest of your life'. Sadly that old saying is invariably true", she told Asha.

Devi decided it was time to take matters into her hands. She had to take a stand. Then one morning, Latika woke up to find Devi sitting patiently waiting for her. Bags lay packed and were lying there in the middle of the hall. She smiled at the shocked Latika and handed her a paper. Latika stared at the sale deed of the house with her mouth open. Devi handed her son a cheque saying "here is the money you wanted. Find yourself a new home as I have done. I will get my things collected shortly. The new owners will move in next month". Devi walked out, head held high.

●●●

30

# Kite in the sky

Floating slowly to the ground, the red and sliver kite closed his eyes and sighed. Plummeting to the ground, he watched the other kites gloat as they glided higher and higher. Cut, bruised and sinking slowly, he called for help.

Not long ago, he was dozing peacefully next to Mangu chacha, watching him rub the thread with the little silvery pounded glass powder that would hold him safe. Faster and faster the hands flew to make the strong sliver blue thread. A smile on his lips, his eyes dropped in deep slumber as if floating in clouds with every swish swish of the hands that moved next to him. Lifted onto the table, Mangu chacha tied the thread, pasted a long silver tail with pretty pink bows and soon he was sitting next to his other friends on the wall. Yellows, greens, blues covered the walls, as the red and silver kite smiled shyly at the cute blushing pink kite with the blue tail on the opposite wall. Pride filled the air as each one prettier than the other, waited eagerly to be a part of the kite flying competition at the village square in the next few weeks. The weeks turned into days as the little kite's frozen eyes stared at the door. One by one the kites squealed with joy and wagged their tails as they got lifted off the rack. And then the big day came. Too late, it's too late now he thought as his tail drooped in disappointment. No one wants me, thought the little red and silver kite as he cowered in the corner his eyes drooped, not daring to look at the rest of the torn and dirty kites on the racks mocking him. Then suddenly tinkle tinkle went the bell, hanging over the door, as little Ramesh and Raju ran into the shop their eager hands lifting the colorful kites and setting them aside. The red and silver kite rattled his tail to draw their attention in desperation and soon the warm breeze was rushing through his tail as the two boys ran through the streets, holding tightly onto the string. They ran past the village well, with bemused smiling women, the village barber, the panchayat office, Mangalsingh, the old dhobhi pulling his donkey. Nothing could stop the boys now, not even the beckoning sweet shop. Onwards they ran, straight to the steps of the tank pushing through the many laughing boys holding on to the string of their kites.

Slowly little Ramesh raised the red, and silver kite off the ground with small tugs, as Raju held onto the string slowly letting it loose. Gulping the warm air, the kite rose to the skies, sticking its tongue out at the green, blue and purple kites, then slowly higher and higher, and soon past Guddu's orange and blue kite. "Look", thought the red and silver kite, "I can see the village streets and look there goes Mangu chacha on his cycle past the post office, and look over there, I can see little Ramesh's house with the goats grazing in the porch. I can even see the village school!" Higher and higher rose the red and silver kite, playing hide and seek with the other kites dancing dangerously close. Swaying away, shaking its tail, he raised his head proudly to the clouds, zipping past the other kites. Confident and growing pompous with every little tug at his string, the red and silver kite smiled as it soared the clear blue skies, as it played tag with the other kites dancing in the breeze when suddenly a violent jerk woke him out of his reverie. "Oh my god", thought the red and silver kite, "where is little

Ramesh and why am I floating to the ground. My string is cut and I am dead", cried the red and silver kite closing its eyes, as it floated down like a feather that had just dropped out of a bird's plume. The warm breeze lifted him past, as he saw the other kites sticking their tongues out at him. "Goodbye, goodbye, you looser", they said crying out to him. Twisting, turning and floating slowly to the ground, he closed his eyes and sighed, as he plummeted to the ground. It watched the other kites gloat as they glided higher and higher. Cut, bruised and sinking slowly, he called for help.

Tangled in the lowest branch of the big banyan tree, slowly the little red and silver kite opened its eyes, as its string twirled itself tightly around and around the branch. "Whew, atleast I'm not torn at all, thank god", it thought swaying in the breeze staring at the sky filled with a rainbow of colorful dancing kites in the blue clear sky. It lay there, up in the branch forlorn, when a small tug at its string shook him free as he stared into the smiling face of Chandu, the dhobhi's son, gently trying to nudge him of the branch. "I'm safe, I'm safe. Careful, careful Chandu, don't tear me please", beamed the little red and silver kite slowly twisting and helping Chandu untangle him as he shook hands with the blue string being tied to its tail. "I will not let you down" promised the red and silver kite, as Chandu ran through the streets of village holding tightly to the string with the warm breeze running through the tail of the red and silver kite, past the village well with bemused smiling women, the village barber sitting under the tree, the panchayat office, Mangalsingh the dhobhi trying to drag his stubborn donkey climb the steps of the tank. Up in the sky the little kite rose, gulping in the warm breeze, smiling as the other kites smirked, challenging him on, as they danced in unison in the beautiful blue sky.

●●●

**31**

# A nonsensical story

The house yawned as the sun rose in the east, stretching its arms out to the sky spreading a warm golden glow. The cat shook itself awake as the windows rattled, and fell off the mantelpiece hitting the floor with a thud and a loud meow. Tail between the legs it ran out into the barn, tripping over pig's pink little outstretched legs slamming into the pole and falling asleep again. The little piggy pulled its legs in and rolled over crushing the little piglets nestling under her as she grunted her way out to the trough, and dipped her flat pointed nose into the water. The little duck flapped around annoyed, as the fat little piggy ran off dripping water on the sleeping black dog on the hay bundles next to the trough. The black dog growled at the piggy as the water splattered on its coat, got up, shook the water off its body, and bounded off running after the sheep in the fields. The sheep ran helter skelter as the dog snapped at their heels, wailing baa baa, scampering up the hillock, while the cows stood in disdain watching them run, as they sat there, chewing at their cud, flicking their tails at the flies buzzing around them. The black crow flew down and sat on the cow's back, skipping up and down as the tail flicked over its back, like a little girl with her skipping rope.

Nipping at its back, the cow's tail hit the crow hard and off the crow flew to the topmost branch of the big tree and cawed and cawed. The brown horse sitting under the tree hit the trunk of the tree with its hoof and watched the crow fly off in fright into the sky. The brown horse dropped its head with a sigh and lay down basking in the shade of the tree watching the hens clucking close by. Cluck-cluck went the hen and its trail of five chicks as they pecked at the ground near the pond. In went a chick, and cheeped pitifully as the mother hen ran along the riverbank, ordering it out. Cheep-cheep went the chick as it clambered onto the floating bark, holding on for dear life as it floated around the pond on the back of the big fish below. The ripples in the water pushed the chick to shore as it fled out of the water, turning its nose up at the big fish circling the pond, diving in and out of the water, as the bright little kingfisher hiding in the reeds watched carefully, ready to strike. Down the kingfisher swooped, and grabbed the struggling big fish and flew back to the reeds to settle down to lunch. Out came the snake and grabbed the little bird in its fangs, as the fish slipped back gratefully into the water. Zigzagging its way through the reeds holding onto the little bird, the snake flipped over a stone and dropped the little bird and hissed in anger watching its prey rise to the highest branch of the tree as the little rabbit hiding in the reeds cowered in fright as the snake rattled past without noticing. The little rabbit jumped into a burrow in the ground down the passages past the worms and the roots, straight into the cellar of the house, jumping around in happiness as a hand picked him up by the ears and carried him up to the room. The rabbit twitched its little whiskers wriggling to get free and dropped to the ground scuttling under the bed as the hand reached out again. The hand chased the rabbit as it ran from one end of the room to the other, down the stairs, tail between the legs out into the barn, tripping over piggy's pink little outstretched legs slamming into the pole and falling asleep next to the cat. The sun set in the west. The house yawned and stretched its arms out to the sky and wrapped up in rays, and sank into the sea and went to sleep.

●●●

32

# Kitchen circus

She lived all alone, and there she was, plonked on the sofa half-asleep. The blue porcelain vase stood on the corner shelf staring at her on the broken down sofa opposite the television, as it flickered dancing pictures. In the kitchen, the small pot sat comfortably next to the big one shinning new, and the pink and green bottles stood smartly in a row on the shelf, like the horses bobbing their heads circling the ring. The washing machine hummed a soft tune playing hoola hoop with the clothes in its belly, gurgling in the warm water. A warm breeze blew the multi-colored curtains as they trapezed higher and higher, reaching up to the ceiling back and forth, teasing the blades of the fan turning faster and faster trying to trap them. The flames of the stove flickered dangerously, dancing in the fan breeze as it held on to the bottom of the big black non-stick pot. The vegetables singed in the pot as the heat rose and screamed out wafts of steam, lifting the lid gently and dropping it back hissing away like a man twirling plates on a stick, throwing them up and catching them as they fall. The water in the vegetables sang a dying song as it turned to steam, and shot out like the cannon ball in the circus ring. "Get off that sofa!" shouted the last drops of water dying out with a hiss as the vegetables slowly cringed to a black mass, coughing up wafts of black smoke, but she did not stir till the smell wafted out into the hall tickling her nose. "What's that stink?" she thought, as her nose curled up to sniff. Oh god, the food is on the stove, she gasped running into the kitchen, her nose crinkling in disgust as she lifted the cover and then baulked. Off went the fire as she lifted the big black non-stick pot, onto the platform with a bang, the big spoon quickly scooped the burnt mess it into the smiling waiting mouth of the dustbin. The dustbin bag cringed and melted as the hot mass hit the bottom.

Her mother always told her to learn to cook and she never listened, but today she was going to prove her wrong. She was not calling for a pizza again. So it was back to the cutting board and as she leaned up to reach out to the unhappy recipe book, it began to flap its pages in despair. The pots on the shelf banged in anticipated despair and the knife wanted to battle the hand that held it as she bent into the fridge to check the tray. The brinjal cringed back as she reached out for it and gasped with relief as she dropped it. "No! No!" screamed the ladyfingers as they were lifted and placed onto the cutting board. Flip flip went the pages of the recipe book, like a trapeze on a swing. The book starred at her in disdain, as she turned the pages frowning in concentration, running her finger down the list of ingredients of each recipe, undecided what to do. "Not this one, she can't possibly manage", thought the book. Flip, flip went the pages again as the warm breeze lifted the smirking curtains peeping over her shoulder. "Aa Ha, this is perfect", she sang "ladyfingers in yoghurt gravy" as she chopped in gay abandon.

Splutter went the condiments, as they jumped up and down in the hot oil gleefully higher and higher trying to outdo each other like a juggler in the ring. In came the ladyfingers, swirling round and round, like a motorbike in the well of death waiting to reach the top. It was going to be okay; "so far so good", they thought, waiting for spinning in their heads to stop. Down came the shower of powdered spices like a cool shower, and the ladyfingers bobbed and merrily rolled around like bears in the circus ring. It was going well, they said as they pranced like the horses in the circus ring, turning a nice greenish brown colour together. They heard her reach for the pot in the fridge, as the cold milk chattered its teeth like clashing cymbals in a band. "Hey wait, you idiot!" shouted the milk, "it's the yoghurt you need". "Put me down," screamed the milk as it gurgled "it's my blanket of cream, look! The yoghurt is in the bowl next to me". The milk grabbed the torn blanket of cream and covered its head in shame, as she scooped it up without a second glance. In went the cream, trying desperately to hang on as she mindlessly covered the milk pot. Banging the fridge door shut, she dug the spoon into the pan. The ladyfingers cringed in horror and hiccupped, gurgled clambering up the sides of the pot trying to escape. "Don't you dare touch me", they screamed to the cream as they clung to the sides trying to get out of the way. The cream now resigned to its fate, decided to have its share of fun, as it ran around the pot trying to cover them with its sticky layer of white, playing a deadly game of catch, scuttling around, as the spoon hula hooped them around. The cream stuck its nose up at the ladyfingers, but soon it was over as they all sank together to the bottom, a mess of green and white. Slowly, everything curdled and the cream shouted to the ladyfingers for help, grabbing onto the spoon and holding on for dear life. She stopped stirring and lifted the spoon, staring in horror at the mess wrapped around it and struggled to shake it off.

She gasped in horror, staring at the gooey mess hanging on for dear life to the spoon. "I've done it again, I've done it again", she said, running out raising her hands in abandon, leaving a deafening silence behind, as the mess in the pot desperately tried to stay afloat and then sank slowly turning cold. The curtains waved a smirking goodbye, and fell back resting against the windows tired as the pages of the recipe book heaved a thankful tearful goodbye to the poor vegetable. The greedy dustbin patted its stomach in anticipation as the mobile sang beep beep beep "one large pizza please" she said, and fell back into the belly of the sofa.

●●●

**33**

# Women driver?

When a friend mentioned to Raaji the other day, that he can't stand two things: one, men dancing and two, women drivers, it got her thinking. A few years ago, very rarely would the male counterpart allow women to touch their precious cars? It was clearly a defined honour to sit next to them, while they drove. She recalled her father getting admitted in hospital with a mild stroke, when Mom said he would never drive again our Dodge car. Raaji always loved that old Morris car of theirs, with its leafy green colour, black cute fenders, and brown seat covers and the 1660 number. For so many years, she had begged permission to drive the car and now, here she was actually being told to learn how to drive. Twenty days later a certified driver, she proudly walked into the hospital and stuck the license under father's haughty nose. Two days later, father was back behind the wheel, driving an angry Raaji. One day, he relented and on an early morning, they drove out to an unused road, with her on the wheel and continuous grilling on which gear to use, and when to brake or not instructions from father. That did it, Raaji was not going to ask him for the car anymore, and who was happier, naturally him. The licence lay in her cupboard for years, her first and last ambition seething in her heart, a car of her own.

Many years after marriage, they bought their first car. She was queen at last of her dream, and refused to let her husband drive her around as he grumbled many a years away. Raaji had got her revenge. It was a woman's car, her car, hers alone!

She had proved all the men in her life wrong, She was good and actually too good for them. She was the safest person to have on the road. Never mind that at times in the beginning days, she used hand signals instead of using the indicators, drove at a tortoise pace, occasionally admiring the scenery on the way, deciding dinner menus in her head, causing blood pressure to drivers behind her always, never look left or right with a route set one way or the other in a straight line. Never mind if she was always singing whilst driving, or enjoying the rain pouring in. And talk to herself, of course she did that too!!

Raaji knew that no one really knew the real driver in her? No way, for if the road was empty then she would speed faster than any race driver. She loved singing louder than ever; maneuvering like a maniac, raising a fist at cab drivers never understanding why they cruise in the middle of the road always. And not to forget those male counterparts talking into their mobiles, flicking their locks, staring in the rear mirror until they spot, her, a woman driver behind. Well! Then suddenly it's a clash of titans, for suddenly the male counterpart breaks out of his slumber, drops his mobile, drops in a few four letter words, steps on the gas and whizzes past, content on having outdone her, 'the woman'. Of course, it's another thing that as soon as he slumbers again, Raaji would step on the gas and zip past a shocked face never to be caught again on the wrong foot.

"Besides, who said speed and rashness belongs to the males? Women are known to conquer space and rule the world – then who dared to question us, the Jhansi Ki Ranis, on the road? We just sometimes let them think that they are masters of the road, because it's that very same insufferable man out there, who will at the end of the day come home to bow to the real master, the women of today- us, their wives!" Raaji smiled with satisfaction as she lovingly patted "Waggy", as she called her car.

www.ingramcontent.com/pod-product-compliance
Lightning Source LLC
Chambersburg PA
CBHW031207260626
47169CB00004B/1272

*9789385665585*